Serena

SAYS

Serena

SAYS

Tanita S. Davis

KATHERINE TEGEN BOOKS
An Imprint of HarperCollins Publishers

Katherine Tegen Books is an imprint of HarperCollins Publishers.

Serena Says
Copyright © 2020 by Tanita S. Davis
All rights reserved. Printed in the United States of America.
No part of this book may be used or reproduced in any manner whatsoever without
written permission except in the case of brief quotations embodied in critical
articles and reviews. For information address HarperCollins Children's Books, a
division of HarperCollins Publishers, 195 Broadway, New York, NY 10007.
www.harpercollinschildrens.com

Library of Congress Cataloging-in-Publication Data

Names: Davis, Tanita S., author.
Title: Serena says / Tanita S. Davis.
Description: First edition. | New York, NY : Katherine Tegen Books, [2020]
| Audience: Ages 8–12. | Audience: Grades 4–6. | Summary: "After her best
friend, JC, has a kidney transplant, Serena feels that they are falling out of
touch, especially as JC makes a new best friend in the hospital"— Provided by
publisher.
Identifiers: LCCN 2020000857 | ISBN 978-0-06-293697-4 (hardcover)
Subjects: CYAC: Best friends—Fiction. | Friendship—Fiction. | Kidneys—
Diseases—Fiction. | Transplantation of organs, tissues, etc.—Fiction. | Video
blogs—Fiction. | African Americans—Fiction.
Classification: LCC PZ7.D3174 Ser 2020 | DDC [Fic]—dc23
LC record available at https://lccn.loc.gov/2020000857

Typography by David DeWitt
20 21 22 23 24 PC/LSCH 10 9 8 7 6 5 4 3 2 1

First Edition

To my sister, Jessica Christina, and to my niece, Fallon, both of whom believe they should have gotten a book dedication long before now.

SERENA|SAYS

What's up, World? It's Friday, and this is *Serena Says*, with your girl Serena St. John. It's been a week since I've seen my best friend, JC, and four days since her surgery to get a new kidney, and today she's finally well enough to have visitors! I—

Gah!

I slam my finger on the stop key, scowling as I almost bump the screen and ruin the perfect lineup of my webcam (my laptop on a stack of books), my background (a plain blue sheet taped in front of my closet door), and my lighting (my bendy desk lamp on the top of my dresser).

Ugh. Another choke. Why is my brain like this? It's like I can't even talk anymore. This is my first vlog, and I just want everything to be right.

My sister, Fallon, makes vlogging look fun, like just looking at the camera and saying whatever. It's not easy, though. I feel weird talking to the camera, and I'm not sure I like how my voice sounds.

No wonder Mr. Van der Ven didn't choose me to be one of 6A's morning announcement reporters this semester. He said reporters for Brigid Ogan's TV news show have to be good at public speaking and not afraid to look the camera in the eye and speak up. My sister said I just need to practice—that everyone has something to say, and I just need to put myself out there. She even said when I get good enough, if I want to, I can upload a vlog of mine onto her streaming channel—since I can't have a channel of my own until I'm over thirteen.

Coughing out the tickle in my throat, I practice to the air.

"Welcome to *Serena Says*! I'm your . . . no, wait." If I were at school, the real me, talking to people I knew, how would I say this? Determined, I restart the camera and sit up straight, staring down into its empty eye.

What's up, World? It's Friday, and this is *Serena Says*. It's been a week since I've seen my bestie, JC, and four days since she got her new kidney, and today she's finally well enough to have visitors.

JC and I have been best friends since I skipped from second grade to fourth. I was the youngest girl in our class that year, and the only black girl too. Even though I was younger and smaller than everyone, JC asked me to eat lunch with her on the first day I was in fourth grade. She dragged me out to the swings to play with her friends, and BOOM! Just like that, we were besties.

We've done everything together ever since.

Since I'm class ambassador for sixth grade Room A, at Brigid Ogan Middle School, when I visit JC, I'll catch her up on all the news and report back to my class on Monday during homeroom on how she's feeling. It's only been a week, and depending on how she's doing, JC might be out of school for six weeks—so I'm super excited to see her when I can!

Um, that's the story for now, but stay tuned for more! This is *Serena Says*, and I'm out.

∽ 1 ∽

AWOL Ambassador

IT HAD BEEN DAYS—a hundred and sixty-eight hours. It *felt* like forever since I'd seen JC.

We'd texted, and I talked to her on the phone every day she hadn't been too woozy, to catch her up on all the news. Since she'd left school in September, she'd missed the social studies movie in the library, and Mrs. Vejar's first boys-against-girls life sciences quiz. I'd missed having someone to eat all of the banana chips out of my trail mix. I'd also missed JC's squeaky laugh, and the way she had to wave her hands around when she said anything.

JC's doctor had finally said she could have visitors after her kidney transplant, and all the fun things I'd planned could finally happen. I'd had to wait till the weekend—Mom worked the three-to-eleven shift at the hospital and didn't have time to take me—but I was still going to be JC's first visitor—from school, anyway. JC's huge Filipino family had been camped out in the hospital since day one. For my visit, I'd matched my fun outfit—black jeans, pink and white headband, pink fleece sweatshirt—to the giant greeting card in the pink envelope signed by the entire class. I also had a glittery, gift-wrapped box in a black and pink polka-dot gift bag, full of all the sorts of things that make a stay in the hospital a little less terrible. It felt like I'd been planning everything forever—but then I started sneezing so much Friday night my eyes watered.

I wasn't going anywhere.

Before JC had even gone to the hospital, she'd explained to our science class how her kidney transplant would work. JC had been given lots of drugs to squash her immune system so her body would accept the new kidney. Some of those drugs JC would have to take for years. The drugs meant that JC's immune system remained too squashed to fight off germs at all, so after surgery she could only have very healthy visitors, one at a time, who washed their hands in sanitizer goo and wore hospital masks over their faces. Even when she got out of the hospital, JC couldn't use public transportation, go to school or church, or even go to the movies for weeks and weeks, until her doctor gave her the all-clear.

People sneezing like their heads were going to fall off should not even think about going near her. So now my mom and Leilani Camacho's mom were going to meet downtown so Leilani could be the class ambassador and drop off the card and gift instead.

It was the *worst*.

Leilani was okay—she joined our class on the fourth day of sixth grade, late because her family had just moved to California from Florida. She was nice enough, and everyone liked her, but she'd hardly been around at all before JC had gone to the hospital. Mom had met Mrs. Camacho at the parent volunteers meeting, so she knew Mrs. Camacho lived close by and would be glad to help. But Leilani wasn't *me*. JC was going to have a stranger from our new school that nobody even really knew coming to visit her. This was worse than awful. This wasn't *fair*.

And on top of everything else, my throat was scratchy and sore, my nose was stuffy, and my ears hurt. Both of them.

"Sorry, kid," Mom said, picking up her car keys. "I know how much you wanted to go. But you can't visit JC in the hospital while you're sneezing, Serena. You're getting a bad cold, and we don't want JC sneezing too."

"I know, I *know*," I muttered, scowling at my handful of tissues.

Mom tugged the gift bag from my grip, wiping the handle with a disinfectant wipe, as if even my fingers were leaking germs. "What's the worst that can happen? You don't get to see JC today, and you miss her a little more. But you can talk to her on the phone or 2Face, and I'm sure the other ambassador will take care of everything," my mother said in a soothing, "Serena, calm down" voice. "She'll let JC know who the gifts are from, and she can give you a call if she has any questions. You can tell her everything."

"Yeah, okay, fine," I mumbled without any enthusiasm.

Mrs. Camacho and Mom would work it out. Mom would tell Leilani everything she needed to know, and Leilani would tell JC who had picked out every single game and book of Mad Libs and color of nail polish. Madison Hughes and Eliana Morales and everyone else from our class would visit JC and catch her up. I would talk to her on my 2Face app like we'd already done since she'd been out of surgery, but it wouldn't be the same. It wouldn't be *me* with my best friend, together like we'd been since the fourth grade.

It wouldn't be the same *at all*.

∂ 2 ∂

Brand-New . . . Who?

"AND THEN LANI'S BROTHERS came in," JC was saying, eyes wide, "and Manny waved, and Kai was like, 'JC, right?' And I could *not* believe he knew my name."

"Well, we go to the same school, and their sister just visited you over the weekend," I pointed out, tilting the phone as I stretched out on the front room couch. The sun had gone, and headlights left smudgy streaks in the dimness as cars drove by. "It would be kind of weird for them to not know."

"Well, I *know that*," JC said, lowering her chin. "But it was still cool."

"It is," I said, not in the mood to argue. "It is cool. They could have waited out in the hall or something, and not even talked to you. It's nice that they came in. They seem, um, . . . nice."

At my agreement, JC's smile returned, and she fiddled with the thin gold necklace she always wore. "They are! They're super nice. Not like most seventh-grade boys."

I didn't really know any seventh-grade boys, so I stayed quiet. Three weeks ago, I wouldn't have thought JC knew any seventh-grade boys either.

JC rushed on, waving her hands. "Get this—Mr. Camacho brought my parents coffee and a bag of custard doughnuts, which was amazing! I couldn't eat anything, but Mrs. Camacho said they'd bring me something when I get an appetite. She is *so* sweet."

I took a quick breath to agree and choked on a cough. I coughed and coughed some more. My voice sounded like a cement grinder with a granite mountain in it. "Sorry."

"You sound like a dog barking," JC said.

"I'm fine," I gasped. "At least I'm not sneezing as much anymore."

I'd been saying that for the last two days. I didn't even have a fever, but Mom wouldn't let me go back to school. So far, my coughing had interrupted the conversation three times now.

"Anyway, that's not even the best thing," JC said. "Dr. Cho says if all the scans look clear, I can go home on Friday!"

"Already?" My voice squeaked, and I cleared my throat to force it back down to normal levels. "That's great!" On the upside, I wouldn't be seeing my bestie with tubes in her nose and stuff. On the downside, I'd missed the whole hospital thing.

"I know, right? If everything stays good, they'll let me come back to school in time for WinterFest!"

"By WinterFest? That's amazing! It's only three mo—" I held my breath as a tickle caught in my throat. It didn't work. The cough exploded out of me, and this time my eyes watered, my nose dripped, and my mom came into the living room with a glass of water.

"Sorry," I croaked to JC again. I slumped against the arm of the couch, trying to feel around for my box of tissues.

"That's okay," JC said, looking worried, as if the germs could get through the phone. "Listen, I should go anyway. Lani's going to call, and we're going to watch *Modern Diva*. It's on in ten."

"What?" I said, my voice crackling. "You watch

Modern Diva? Since when?"

"Oh, I started binge-watching past episodes last week. Lani and Ginger caught me up on the story line. It's completely addicting."

"Oh," I said kind of stupidly. Leilani watched *Modern Diva* too? I cleared my throat and gave a fake cough. "Well, I should go too. Mom's probably going to say I should rest my voice before I keep doing practice vlogs anyway."

"You probably should," JC said. "Later, Gator."

"Yeah, bye."

I stared at the blank screen on the phone, not really seeing it.

I know my bestie. She doesn't like trash TV. She doesn't like talking on 2Face while she's trying to watch something. Or, at least, she *didn't*.

Who knows what JC likes now? Maybe she got more than a new kidney at the hospital. Maybe she got a new personality too.

Huh.

SERENA|SAYS

[sneeze]

What's up, World? It's Friday. Today—[coughing]

What's up, World? It's your girl Serena St. John, and today on *Serena Says*, we're going to talk about things to do when you're bored!

No . . . that's stupid, and my voice sounds fuzzy. I delete, scowling, and try again.

What's up, World? It's morn— Delete. Restart.

What's up, World? It's Serena.

[coughs]

You know what, World? Actually, it is NOT a good morning. This morning BITES.

It's Friday.

That's all I've got.

It's Friday, World, and this is *Serena Says*, broadcasting from Planet Sick, population 1.

I hate sneezing. I hate coughing.

I would like to be able to BREATHE out of my NOSE again someday. I would like a sense of SMELL. Is that too much to ask, World?

[glares into camera]

This is *Serena Says*, and that's my story.

3

Grumpy Burrito

BETWEEN THIS STUPID COUGH and Leilani getting to visit JC before I do *again*, I'm a sour, cranky grump. It's not like it's Leilani's fault that JC's decided they're friends. JC's friendly like that. In the fourth grade, she just picked me out of nowhere to be her bestie. Maybe she'd had another bestie before me and I didn't see it. Maybe someone was sour and cranky with me and I never knew.

It's not like Leilani isn't nice either. Mom and I met Leilani and her mom at the store once, and Leilani wasn't weird about seeing me; she waved and said hi like normal. At school, she's good at sports and offers to share her food at lunch. She doesn't even make a little face like JC does when Mom packs me vegan corn dogs. But Leilani's also one of those people who knows *everything*. And I mean everything. Mr. Van calls on her like five times a day, and she's always raising her hand.

She's always prepared.

She's always polite.

All the teachers like her.

I have no reason to not like her. None at all, except that it seems like JC likes her . . . more than me. Maybe.

You know what makes things worse when you're miserable? Annoying siblings.

Fallon burst into my room, braids flying, a millisecond after barely knocking once.

"Ree? Where are my metallic paint markers?"

"I don't know," I said, and pulled my blankets up to my shoulders. "I don't have your markers." Fallon's in eighth grade, and she's always losing stuff and blaming me—everything except her phone, which is, like, glued to her hands.

"How do you know you don't have them? You didn't even look," Fallon accused. She walked to my desk and opened the top drawer.

I scowled. "I don't have to look. I didn't borrow them. Get out of my desk."

"Yes, you did," Fallon said, opening another drawer and looking through my pen tray. "I distinctly remember seeing them next to your stuff in the dining room, like, a week ago."

"I was doing homework at the table. *You* were doing something else . . . with your markers. Did you look in the dining room?"

Fallon didn't answer. She just slammed my desk drawer and whooshed out of the room.

"Close the door!" I yelled, but of course she didn't.

Of course, yelling also made me cough again.

"Arf, arf," Mom said, tightening her ponytail as she stood in my doorway.

"Ha-ha," I said. "Could you shut my door?"

"I could," my mother said.

I groaned. My mother is sometimes a *serious* pain. "Fine. *Would* you shut my door, please?"

"In a minute. How's JC this afternoon?"

"Oh, she's fine, just fine—she's great," I lied, not really knowing how she was doing at all. I'd texted her a couple of times but had only gotten one-word answers.

"That's good to hear," Mom said, smiling warmly as my conscience twinged. "Are you hungry? I can warm you up some tomato soup."

"Meh," I said.

"Your other choice is carrot," Mom said. "That's all we have for soup, unless you want to eat rice pilaf and salmon with us. There's kale."

"Ugh," I said again, and rolled over, winding my blanket around me to mummy tightness. Kale is fine, but I hate fish worse than anything.

"Well, you need to eat something," Mom persisted. "You can't hole up here all afternoon like a grumpy burrito."

"Why not?"

My mother sighed. "Wash your hands, straighten up your hair, and come down to the table, please," she said, as if she hadn't heard. "Five minutes." She moved to close the door.

I groaned and rolled to the edge of the bed.

"And ditch the blanket," Mom swung open the door again to add.

My voice rose to a whine. "I'm *cold*."

"And I'm *old*," Mom whined back. "We all have problems. Put on a sweater and some thick socks. Four minutes, Serena."

Just once, I'd like to have the last word talking to my mother. Just *once*.

∽ 4 ∽

Everybody Loves Lani

CLOUDS HUGGED THE TOPS of the brown hills like a puffy white sweater the Thursday Mom finally let me go back to school. It was the first week of October, and it looked like it might rain again, which would be great for our dry California town. At school, everyone was buzzing with the energy that cooler weather brought. During morning announcements, I learned that it was 6A's turn to organize the Friday morning student assembly, which we have every week from seven forty-five to eight fifteen. Mr. Van, who knows I'm trying to get better at public speaking, tried to assign me a part. That is, until he heard my creaky, croaky, crackling voice.

"I can see you're going to be whispering for a while," said Mr. Van. "I had you down to lead the pledge, but we'll just ask someone else."

Nobody really *wants* to talk at student assembly, except kids like Beth Morgan, who wants to be an actress, and Harrison Ballard, who just likes to hear the sound of his voice. But Mr. Van is the nicest teacher I've ever had, and I like him. Plus, he marks participation points toward our citizenship grade, which is the real reason I wouldn't let him bench me.

"I can do it, Mr. Van. I'm okay," I said. My voice was rough and croaky.

"You sound *terrible*," Mr. Van said. "Rest your voice, Serena. Leilani can lead the pledge."

Oh no she couldn't. I waved my hands. "But I'm fine!" I said, way too loudly. My voice cracked but came through okay. "I promise you, Mr. Van, I'm getting better. I'll be ready."

By Friday, when the rain came, I wasn't so sure. First of all, wet weather makes thick, short hair curl up, and mine was so bad, I wanted to wear a hat. I pulled my hair into double buns instead and put on the widest headband I could find. I didn't feel very ready, but at least I looked cute.

My coughing is always worse in the morning, so by the time I got to school I was not only crackly, my voice now sounded lower than Mr. Arsdale's, who drove the bus. When it was time, we lined up and went into the auditorium, sitting in the same order as we lined up—alphabetically. I was near the back of the line, between Liz Simms and Corina Talkington. The 6B class filled the rest of the chairs in our section, mostly quietly. The room grew louder as the seventh and eighth graders filed in. Finally, Mrs. Henry, her yellow suit contrasting brightly against her deep brown skin, walked out onto the platform. It was time to begin with the pledge.

Unfortunately, there was a tickle in my throat.

Walking up the aisle to the front of the auditorium seemed like a long, long way. "Please rise for the pledge," I tried to say when I got there.

First, my voice came out a dry, scratchy hiss, deepening into a barking cough.

I sucked in a breath . . . and coughed. And then I coughed some more.

Oh no.

I could imagine the visual: Shiny face. Snotty nose. Streaming eyes. So *not* a good look.

I tried to speak. Each time I tried, I coughed. Each time I coughed, Mr. Van winced.

Then—oh, the worst, most embarrassing thing of all: Ms. Aagaard, our school nurse, came up and *escorted me* off the stage, putting her arm around me.

"Let's get you some water," she said in a comforting voice.

I tried to tell her I was okay, but I. Could. Not. Stop. Coughing.

Right when I walked past him, Luis Archega made a stupid-sounding seal bark.

Arf! Arf!

A wave of giggles spread as somebody from the back of the room started barking too. As kids from sixth and seventh joined in, Luis barked again, but this time Mr. Van stood in the aisle right next to him. Across the room, Fallon, who usually acted like I didn't exist at school, gave Luis her famous Death Glare while Luis's older brother, Roberto, glared at *her*. Luis didn't even notice all that going on, though, because Mr. Van was standing right next to him, giving Luis *his* Death Glare, and his meant *business*.

"Ladies and gentlemen, where are your manners?"

Mrs. Henry leaned toward the microphone, looking over her glasses.

I was coughing too hard to say anything, but even though my eyes were watering, I gave Luis a Death Glare too.

Gah! This was *so* embarrassing.

The doors of the auditorium swung shut on Mrs. Henry announcing that once everyone else was excused, the sixth grade would be sitting in silence for five minutes to think about respecting others. Then she announced that *she* would lead the pledge.

At least it wasn't Leilani.

SERENA|SAYS

What's up, World? It's Saturday. It's your girl Serena St. John, and this is *Serena Says*.

[sneeze]

Shout out to Brigid Ogan Middle School, which is getting ready for WinterFest! WinterFest is our first all-school show of the school year. It has all the things— music by the Brigid Ogan orchestra and jazz choir, arts and crafts, face painting and carnival games and amazing food. There's a big raffle, and each class raises money for a charity, so people buy holiday gifts like candy and wrapping paper and stuff that supports the school.

Class ambassadors like me usually help with Winter-Fest fundraising. I missed our first bake sale, but our class treasurer, Eliana, told me Temporary Ambassador Leilani was amazing. She didn't just buy poster board and make a few signs for brownie prices, she put prices on an LED board in lights. JC told me Leilani said she assigned people food, too—like vegan and gluten-free treats—and put them all on their own table. Five minutes later? Sold out.

Great, right? I mean, awesome, the bake sale raised tons of money. It's just . . . could Leilani not be perfect, for just, like, five minutes? She makes me feel like a dork.

Can you imagine her coughing to death in front of the whole school? Uh, NO. Some people are—

"What, Mom?"

"No, I'm filming my vlog! And I'm SICK!"

[sigh]

This is *Serena Says*, and our WinterFest segment will be back in just a bit . . . because apparently even if you're DYING around here, you have to clean your room.

∼ 5 ∼

One-Woman Show

"SERENA, OH MY GOSH!" JC whisper-shrieked from my speaker phone.

"What?" I said, parting a section of my hair to make a twist. This was the second time I'd spoken to JC this cloudy Sunday afternoon, but that was normal for us. Our all-time record is seventeen calls and fifty-five texts in one day.

JC was speaking in exclamation points, her voice rising with excitement. "You would not *believe* what just happened! To *me*! At my *house*! Just *now*!"

I coiled the hair and twisted the end. "Yeah? What happened? Did your dad bring you something cool?"

"No! Kai Camacho just came over. To my house.

Just now, Serena! Like, two minutes ago!"

My jaw dropped. I let my twist spin apart as my fingers went slack. "By *himself*?"

"No, he was with his mom. Mrs. Camacho's book club brought Mom some books and a scarf. Wasn't that sweet of them?"

It *was* pretty nice. As far as I knew, my mom wouldn't ever do something like that. For one thing, she didn't have a book club. She always said she didn't have time to read, much less breathe, since Fallon and I took up all the air. "So Kai came with his mom to see you?"

"Well, actually, he stayed in the car," JC admitted. "But he waved through the window. Mrs. Camacho says he thinks he's getting a cough."

"JC!" I laughed so hard my giggles turned to a cough. I caught my breath, then groped through my hair to begin my twist again. "Kai Camacho came to visit your *front yard*, you dork. I was all excited thinking seventh-grade boys were visiting you."

"Well he *would* have," JC rushed on defensively. "He's got a *tickle*. Oh, and guess what else?" she added. "Lani and I found a project for WinterFest!"

I rolled my eyes and parted another section of hair. JC can be a tiny bit competitive when it comes to our class. "Another project?" I asked. "You know we only have to do one."

"What do you mean another project?" JC sounded confused. "I haven't been at school to pick even one, remember?"

I twisted the hair and clipped it down, so my style would stay. "Yeah, I know, but a way long time ago, we decided we were going to make a birdbath with your dad. Remember?"

"Oh, that," JC said dismissively. "I had a better idea. Lani went on Artistly and found these super-cute felt owls with beaded feathers. We're going to make fridge magnets out of them."

"Wait, what?" I blurted. "JC, that'll take, like, five minutes. What about the birdbath?"

"You can still come over and make a birdbath with my dad if you want," JC said generously. She always shared her father, since mine left Mom and Fallon before I was even born. "He could probably do it next week or something, only I don't think you can make stuff with cement if it's raining."

"I don't want to do a project with your *dad*," I protested. I didn't like how small and hurt my voice sounded. "How could you have spaced on this? We planned out everything!" We'd talked about it for days. First, we'd tint the cement with powdered paint, and then put marbles around the edges in a wave pattern. It would have been gorgeous, and it also would have made serious money at the raffle.

"Serena." JC sighed. "I'm sorry, okay? I totally forgot about the bath thingy we were going to do, because Lani was talking about magnets and I got excited. Those owls are adorbs!"

I sighed back, disappointment lowering my voice. "Fine. I can make magnets, I guess."

JC didn't say anything for a long moment.

I stifled the urge to cough and cleared my throat instead. "JC? Hey, are you still there?"

"Yeah. Um, Serena," JC began, her voice a little odd, "you can make magnets if you want to, but, maybe just flamingos or something, all right? 'Cause . . . Lani and I have dibs on owls, all right? And Kai's probably going to be helping us, so you'll have to make something else or we'll have too many of one thing."

"Oh," I said, my stomach shrinking. At Winter-Fest, parent volunteers sell the extra donations that don't fit into the raffle baskets to raise money for individual classes. That wasn't what JC meant by "too many," though. She meant that any owl magnets

I made would be too many, even if it was just one.

I didn't know what to say. It hurt too much that she was choosing Leilani over me. And Kai—why did she have to be so weird about Kai? It wasn't like they were *actually* going out or anything. Was he *really* going to hang out with them and glue little magnets onto felt owls?

"You'll find tons of other magnet projects if you look on Artistly," JC told me. "Lani says that's where you get the best ideas for everything."

Oh, right, *Lani says* it, so it must be true.

"Fine. Whatever," I said, and pressed my lips together so I couldn't let out one more word.

It used to be that the best ideas JC and I had came from putting our heads together in a brainstorm. Since that's not what *Lani says*, though, I guess that's just not true anymore.

6

Punctured

MY MOTHER SAID THAT sixth-grade friendships change, and change was beyond our control, and we shouldn't take it personally. She said that the best thing that could happen to me was that I find out how to pick a project and stand on my own. I don't even know what she meant by that. I *do* stand on my own. And I had a *perfectly good birdbath project.*

And now I don't.

Fallon got online and found some bird feeders made out of paper towel rolls and wooden spoons, which were totally lame—and I said thank you, but no thank you. Mom got online and found bird nests made from chocolate-coated cornflakes with little chocolate-covered almonds in them for eggs.

Which, hello? Also lame. People do those for Easter, not Christmas.

"Thanks, Mom, but no," I said, turning away from the picture on her phone.

"Well, that's all I've got, kid," Mom said, pulling on a white lab coat over her purple nursing scrubs, "so I'm going to finish getting ready for work. You'll find something, Serena. I have faith in you."

Oh, goody, Mom had *faith* in me. I didn't need faith; I needed A WINTERFEST PROJECT. Like, *right* now. WinterFest was only eight weeks away. It was hopeless! I was never going to find anything.

At least I had a new book bag. My *bibi*, which is what I call my grandmother, sent it to me as a little present, since she'd heard I'd been sick so early in the school year. My bag was black with fat pink roses on it, and two little outside pockets—so, so cute—and a little tiny mini-backpack that fit inside! It was so cute it almost made me a little less grumpy. *Almost.*

After announcements Tuesday morning, Mr. Van reminded the class officers that there was going to be a meeting during lunch. At the 11:50 bell, the six of us—our president, VP, treasurer, secretary, social secretary, and me, class ambassador, wandered out to grab extra snacks from the vending machine or lunch from the cafeteria. Instead of finding a table with the rest of the mob of sixth graders, we trooped back into Mr. Van's room.

I was already opening my zip bag of sliced apples as Eliana wheeled along next to me in her chair, telling me about the new graphic novel she'd just read. Then Eliana stopped. She pushed up her glasses and frowned.

"Uh-oh."

"What?" I asked, looking up.

Leilani was already sitting at the table in the corner of the classroom, her mouth full of sandwich. Her eyes widened, and she flushed as I stared at her. I crumpled my bag of apples in my fist.

Well, this wasn't at all *super* awkward.

I shifted my lunch bag and crossed my arms. "Um, Leilani . . . ? What are you doing here?"

Leilani chewed as fast as she could, holding up a hand for me to wait until she could speak. Finally, she choked down her bite and stood, pushing back her straight black hair. "Serena! You're here!"

Eliana and I looked at each other. I'd been back at school now for four days. "Uh . . ."

Leilani waved her hand again. "No, I mean, I

thought you were sick again after all that coughing at assembly. I told Mr. Van an idea I had for a Harvest Party, and he called this meeting so I could tell everyone, and, um . . ." Leilani trailed off and shrugged, running her hand over her hair like she was flustered.

"Don't worry about that," Mr. Van said, rescuing her. "Serena, come on in and sit down. Lani's got an exciting idea, and we've got room for both of our ambassadors in this meeting."

BOTH of our ambassadors? BOTH, as in *two*?

I looked at Eliana, but this time she was looking at her fingernails.

"Mr. Van . . . there's only one class ambassador," I reminded him.

"We can have two, can't we?" Mr. Van asked. He raised his eyebrows, sending me silent messages as the light above his head glinted off of his bald spot. Mr. Van's eyebrows said, *Say yes, Serena. Come sit down, Serena. Be a good sport, Serena.*

I *wanted* to. I *wanted* to be a good sport and do what Mr. Van wanted . . . but Leilani Camacho had already taken my spot as class ambassador once. Then she took my birdbath partner. She wasn't getting anything else—Not. One. Thing.

"No," I said. The word dropped out of my mouth and plopped on the floor.

Beside me, Eliana sucked in a breath.

My face felt hot and tight. I felt too many feelings, and they all wanted to come out at once.

"No?" Mr. Van repeated, a worried little line between his eyebrows. "We can't have two ambassadors . . . ? Are you sure?"

I looked at Leilani, who was looking at the floor, twisting a hank of her hair into a rope. I looked at Mr. Van, who was leaning against his desk, his expression unhappy.

Wait. This wasn't *my* fault. We didn't *have* two ambassadors! The class only voted for *one*! Wasn't Leilani going to say something? Wasn't Mr. Van going to do something? Why was everybody looking at *me*?

I smelled hot food and our class president, Erik Peterson, came up behind me carrying a cafeteria lunch of lasagna and french bread. He already had his baby carrots in his mouth, like walrus tusks. "I'm here! Let's get this party started," he said like he always did.

But this time, nobody laughed. The moment stretched too tight, like an overinflated balloon.

"What did I miss?" Erik asked, his blue eyes wide. "What's going on?"

"Well . . . ," Mr. Van began.

"I quit," I tried to say. But the balloon popped, and instead of words, I got tears ready to explode all over the place. I put my head down and got out of there.

SERENA|SAYS

What's up, World? It's your girl Serena! Welcome back to my vlog. Today, let's check out WHAT'S IN MY BAG!

[holds up bag]

So this is my bag, which is technically a teensy backpack that fits into the big backpack that I take to school. It's actually a crossbody bag, but if you go like THIS—

[clips the straps to the back]

Ta-DAH! New backpack. I know, cute, right? This sea turtle charm I got from when we went to Florida. I LOVE it, because sea turtles are my favorite thing after owls. Wait, no, actually, after hedgehogs. And tiny frogs. Um, anyway, moving on—

When you open my bag, the first thing you see is my PLANNER, which my mother gave me this year for the first day of school. I had to, um, rip out pages, so there's nothing much written in it yet, except on the first page, where Mom wrote my name and all my classes. I think she thought I would write homework assignments in there, but assignments are on Pegasus—our school message board—so . . . The pages I tore out just had some stuff I'd planned to do with JC, which is kind of not happening now because she's maybe too busy with OTHER people, so . . .

Anyway! The next thing in my purse is my glasses case that holds my sunnies, which are super cute and very helpful to wear when I don't want people to look at me. Sunnies are very important if your eyes are red for any reason, like crying through most of lunch because someone just thought they could roll up and take your class ambassador job, and everyone acted like that was JUST FINE. Um . . . okay, so, here in my first right zipper pocket is the space for my phone. I keep an extra flexipod in there to hold my phone, just in case I need to make a vlog real quick.

Oh, and the SECOND zipper pocket on the right side has this little stripy bag, which is stuff for Lady Days. And before you say anything, FACT: Lady Days happen to, like, half of the population. SECOND FACT: Even if you're gender identified to be NOT in that half of the population? You still need to respect the Lady Days. There's nothing embarrassing about bodies and how they work, and everybody has blood, right? So today's *Serena Says* PSA: Lady Days are a Thing. No shame, no shade—deal with it.

Um, okay. Back to my bag. In my left zipper pocket is my hand sanitizer, which is lavender and smells AMAZ-ING. There's my pack of tissues, which I used half of at lunch. There's a tinted lip balm with SPF in raspberry pink, and a compact mirror my uncle Ron brought back for me from Scotland. I know, the thistle is ADORABLE! Even though he says he got it for me because I'm prickly, which, WHATEVER, Uncle Ron. Seriously.

There's a little travel-size deodorant for pit emergencies, my pick-comb, because you NEVER, ever, ever, EVER just brush natural curls, EVER. Unless you're using an old toothbrush and smoothing out your baby hairs. Um . . . I think that's—no wait. There's an extra scrunchy and a headband—because BIG HAIR needs backup gear, and—OH!!! There's my lace headband! I thought I had lost it!

Wow—note to self: clean out purse more often.

So, that's it! That's what's in Serena's bag! Tell me, people—what's in YOUR bag? Am I missing something important here? Do you have a pack for Lady Days? Or, heck, maybe you have a bag for Dude Days? What ARE Dude Days? Serena says what you carry tells people a lot about you—so make sure it's organized—and keep it cute.

That's my story, and I'm out . . .

And yay! Except for scratching my forehead and that weird face I made about Uncle Ron, this vlog was almost perfect! I think I'm almost ready to start posting these.

7

Last-Second Solutions

ON FRIDAY, JUST AFTER the seventh graders introduced our guest speaker, our vice-principal, Mrs. Henry, announced that she needed to see the following people after student assembly: Harrison Ballard, Cameron Jones, Serena St. John, Hyung Kim, Eliana Morales, Ally Leonard, and Sunita Trivedi.

I tried to concentrate on Mr. Anderson's talk about volunteering at the wildlife museum but couldn't. I wasn't sure what Mrs. Henry wanted, but I was pretty sure I wouldn't like it.

Mrs. Henry is . . . particular. She's stylish, like my bibi. Mrs. Henry always wears a suit with matching shoes, so she's all in one color. And, like Bibi, she always has her reading glasses on the end of her nose, but never looks through hers. She does stuff like using beets to make pink cupcake frosting instead of just a tiny drop of food coloring—because food coloring is *terrible* for you, and beets are *good*. She also brings her juicer to school during test week and hands out little paper cups of celery and carrot juice between classes.

FYI, carrot juice tastes like what would happen if you let construction paper, white glue, and a lot of sugar soak together in a cup of water, and then drank it.

It's dis-gust-ing.

I also knew I probably wouldn't like whatever it was Mrs. Henry wanted me for, because she wanted Harrison Ballard too. Harrison is . . . a lot. He's always been the biggest boy in our class, but coming back from summer this year, he's now five foot eleven—so he's big *and* tall and *loud*, with huge brown curls and brushy eyebrows and light-brown skin. He wears plaid shirts every day and has been carrying a briefcase since the second grade. He used to pick his nose, but now he just rubs his nose on his sleeves, which in my opinion is not any less gross.

Harrison likes to lean his elbow on my head,

because, he says, I'm a short little Hobbit, like those small, half-human people who lived underground in the Tolkien books my mom likes. Which—whatever—not everyone can be a giant boy mutant. JC is just a little taller than I am, but Harrison never bothers *her*. JC says it's because Harrison loves me so much there's nothing in his briefcase but little pieces of paper with my name on them. She says she saw them.

That isn't funny. That's *creepy*.

I hope JC's just kidding.

Student assembly had barely ended before Harrison was standing in the aisle next to my seat. He stared down expectantly. "Well, Hobbit?"

"I'm not talking to you, Harrison," I mumbled, getting up.

Harrison followed me up the aisle anyway. "I didn't know you joined Student Senate."

It took four steps before Harrison's words made it into my brain. "What?"

Harrison loomed over me. "Student Senate," he said, adding, "man, you're short."

"I'm not short, I'm just not a mutant giant," I told him like I always do. "And what do you mean, Student Senate?"

Harrison peered into my eyes and gently knocked his big knuckled fist against my forehead. "Hello? Is anyone in there?"

I ducked away, intending to return a fist to his squishy stomach with considerably more force, but Mrs. Henry's, *"Ladies and gentlemen,"* in her zero-tolerance voice straightened me up fast. I jumped away from Harrison like he was on fire.

Not that it made any difference, since he followed me down to the front of the auditorium and sat right next to me.

Sigh.

Mrs. Henry listened as Sunita called roll, declared that we had a quorum, and sat back in her seat. Our vice-principal looked at us over her gold-rimmed glasses.

"Thank you, everyone. Serena, this is your first time serving with our senate group, so I want to especially make you welcome. This is a big responsibility, but I know you're up to it." Mrs. Henry gave me a pointy little smile, which probably meant that I should be quiet and nod, but my hand raised without consulting my brain.

"What is it, Serena?" Mrs. Henry's brows raised.

"Excuse me, Mrs. Henry, but I'm not *on* the

senate. I don't know—"

"Mr. Van felt that since you've been such a big help as a class ambassador, you'd be a valuable addition to our senate body."

Or, which was more likely, Mr. Van was trying to make me feel better for letting Leilani take my job. My voice rose. "Mrs. Henry, I don't know anything about being a senator! Mr. Van didn't even ask! I—"

Mrs. Henry cut in. "This is an opportunity, Serena, for a young lady like yourself to stand up and speak out. I know you can do it. If you have further questions, why don't you see me after the meeting? We only have a few minutes, and while this is not an official senate session, the best thing you can do to learn about how we do things here is just to watch, all right?"

But . . . but . . . I swallowed the words, seeing the other students eyeing Mrs. Henry and me with nosy interest. Grinding my teeth, I gave in, giving Mrs. Henry a short nod.

"Thank you. Now, let's hear how preparations are going for our Red Ribbon Week this month. Ms. Chairman? You have the floor."

I ignored Sunita as she talked, fuming. Mr. Van is *not* my favorite teacher anymore, and I don't like

43

Mrs. Henry at *all*. Brigid Ogan has way too many special events—everyone is so *over* Red Ribbon Week. Also, Student Senate is *pointless*. Last year, Fallon helped revise the Brigid Ogan Student Constitution when she was a seventh-grade senator. She acted like having a constitution made a difference, when everyone knows that teachers and Mrs. Henry are the ones who make the rules. I hate it when teachers pretend that what kids want matters. Adults do *not* listen.

"And, Serena, maybe you and Harrison can head up the Student Participation subcommittee," Sunita was saying. "Ally had a great idea that we can run it like a second Spirit Week, with crazy sock days and stuff like that." Sunita looked at me. "Just brainstorm a week's worth of ideas and be ready to present them at the regular meeting."

What?

I was still trying to figure out where it all went wrong when the meeting was over. Harrison picked up his briefcase and walked out of the auditorium.

"Wait," I blurted, hurrying after him. "I don't even know what a subcommittee is! And what's a quorum?"

Harrison shook his head. "Serena," he said patiently, "the best thing you can do to learn about how we do things on Student Senate is just to watch, all right?"

I punched as fast as I could, but I still missed. Harrison's mutant giant laugh echoed down the hall. *Ha-ha-ha!*

Dork.

8

Sipping with the Enemy

"DO EITHER OF YOU know the answer to number thirteen?"

I was on 2Face again, doing homework with JC and Leilani. Hearing a murmur from the other person in the room, I scanned to the top of my paper and answered out loud. "Sure, JC . . . I got 148.04."

There was a pause—a long one, where I could only see the top of JC's head. She was probably doing the problem again and checking my answer against her own.

Sure enough, the next thing she said was "That's not right."

"It's right. I multiplied it out again. I'm doing all the division problems first, and then—"

"Yeah, but Lani says it's 148. You're supposed to round it to the nearest tenth."

I grimaced. "I *know that*. If you'd let me finish, I was going to say that I was doing all the division problems first, then going back and doing the rounding."

"That's not how I would do it," Leilani's voice sounded tinny through the speaker.

JC agreed, sounding anxious like she always did about math. "Yeah, Serena. What if you forget? Then they're *all* wrong."

I sighed. How many times did we have to do this? "I won't forget. I have it written down as a step. That's what Mr. Van said to do—to break up a problem and do it in steps, remember?"

"Uh-huh." JC sounded distracted, and I swallowed a sigh. JC and I did homework on 2Face a lot even before her surgery and everything. If I couldn't be right there with her, it was the next best thing. I didn't know how she'd done it as a three-way call, though. That was some kind of paid service, and Fallon and I could only have the free one. Still, since JC hated math, her parents got her all the help they could get. And it helped her to talk to me AND Leilani. Even though I could barely hear Leilani's voice, I felt upset and ignored, but I was trying my best not to be a baby about it. JC was my best friend. If doing math with both of us helped JC understand it better, I wouldn't be a good best friend if I complained.

Right?

After a long moment, JC spoke again. "Have you done any word problems?"

"Eew, no," I jumped in. "I wish Mr. Van wouldn't give us so many of those. Twelve for one assignment is ridiculous."

"I know, right? Okay, Lani says the first one is—"

"Wait, don't tell me!" I exclaimed. "I can do it!" *I* didn't need math help, especially not from Leilani Camacho, no matter how smart Mr. Van thought she was.

"Well, hurry up," JC said. "We're almost done, and Lani did the word problems first."

"How are you almost done?" I complained. "I'm on fifteen, and didn't you just ask me about thirteen?"

"Lani's done, and I'm almost done," JC repeated. "And I'm going to hang up pretty soon. Lani's mom brought boba tea, and I want mine."

I looked up from my paper. "Wait. Leilani's at your house? Right now?"

JC's face came back into focus, and she panned the camera around. "Look, she's right here. I told you she was going to do math with us!"

I opened my mouth to say I wished JC had invited *me* over, then bit my tongue. I didn't want to sound pathetic. "I know, I just thought . . ." I shook my head. Boba and homework help and Leilani. And here I was, at home with my water bottle, doing problems all on my own. "Um, never mind. I'll talk to you later."

"Okay, I'll call you tonight. Ooh! There are these little crepe things you'd like, Serena! I'll have to ask Mrs. Camacho how to make them. Oh—listen, Lani says to tell you she'll call you later."

She will? I said a hurried goodbye, but JC had already ended our session.

I hadn't said anything to Leilani Camacho since the Thursday Mr. Van gave her my class ambassador job. As far as I'm concerned, we don't need to talk to each other ever.

Leaving behind my word problems, I wandered into the living room. I found the distraction I was looking for sitting on the couch and playing a game on her phone.

"Hey, Flea? What are we doing for Halloween?"

My sister didn't look up. She's doing this thing where she ignores Mom and me when we use her baby name. I kind of don't blame her, though; Mom called me "Rena-Beana" for *ages*.

I sighed loudly. "Fallon?"

"What?" She looked up at last.

"Halloween. It's coming up soon. What are we doing?"

"Who's this 'we'?"

I rolled my eyes. Jeez, my sister was so annoying. "You know what? Never mind."

Fallon smirked down at her phone. "Sharyn and Laine and I are going to the corn maze at Arden-wood."

I sighed and wandered into the kitchen. Last year, Mom worked on Halloween, so Fallon went to NewPark Mall's haunted house in her Hogwarts robe, while JC and I ordered pizza and watched a movie while we handed out candy. JC liked handing it out in our neighborhood, because unless all her little cousins came over, there weren't enough kids in hers. That night, Fallon and her friend Sharyn crashed our party like an hour into the movie. Even though they made fun of what we were watching (*The Dark Crystal* is the best movie ever, and my sister has *zero* taste) and ruined what was supposed to be our private pizza party, Sharyn gave us facials and crazy manicures, and Fallon brought out her colored chalk and we all striped our hair. We let them eat the rest of our pizza for that.

I couldn't help but think that Halloween this year wasn't going to be anywhere near as fun. Not with JC stuck at home, not even getting to hand out candy. Not with Leilani hanging around.

So Leilani was supposed to call me tonight. I scowled as I rummaged in the kitchen cupboard for Mom's tin of Godiva. If I had to chitchat with the enemy, I needed hot chocolate.

SERENA|SAYS

I need to find theme music that's exactly six seconds long . . . I don't like this one. Anyway.

What's up, World? It's Saturday, and—

[loud vacuum cleaner noises from the behind the door]

FALLON!!!

[vacuum grows louder]

FALLON! I'M PICKING YOU UP ON THE MIC!

[door opens]

I'M TRYING TO PRACTICE MY VLOGGING!

[vacuuming pauses, continues another few seconds, then stops for good]

What's up, World? It's the weekend, and it's time for another *Serena Says* STORYTIME!

Welcome back to my vlog!

JC's been on my mind, so it's time for a best friend story . . . Did I ever tell you about the time JC and her family took us to Gilroy Gardens and we totally danced in a Memorial Day parade? It is one of the MOST JC things to have ever happened in the history of our friendship, and it's SO her.

SO. We were in the fourth grade—I was nine, and JC was going to be ten—and JC had begged and begged and begged her parents to take us to Gilroy Gardens because she wanted to ride the rides there and see the giant puzzle trees and all that. And so, the park had just opened for the season, and the sun was out, and it was all gorgeous and everything. Gilroy Gardens Main Street had this whole thing for Memorial Day—you know, marchers with flags, and this whole dance troupe in costume and a band with drums and flutes and whatnot. And so we get there, and everybody is lining up on the parade route, and I was still SUPER short back then, and so Mr. Gerardo told me to get right out front of everyone, and we stood and watched the parade. They were amazing—there were all of these dancers and gymnasts, and people with flags and people doing cartwheels, and I was THERE for it, right? I mean, I'm standing out in the best spot on the whole parade route, I'm with my best friend, and I am INTO it.

So, they had some, I guess, square dancers? They were dancing in pairs, and they were, I don't know, kind of galloping along, doing these steps, and people were kind of clapping along with the music, and then they would kind of split up and dance with someone from the crowd, right? And I thought, "Oh, that's cool, the people in the crowd are part of the parade too." Then, all of a sudden, they were in front of me! And this guy held out his hand for me, and I took it, and he spun me around, just danced me around, and suddenly, I was a part of the parade. It was AMAZINGLY cool. It was SO fun. I totally could not dance, but he just kind of spun me around and pretty much held me up off the ground. All I know is, it went by fast, and then he kind of turned me around, and set me down, and boom—he was gone.

And I had NO idea where I was.

I mean, duh, I was at Gilroy Gardens, and I was on the parade route. But the guy who had danced with me had kind of screwed up, and he hadn't danced me back to where I'd been. He'd danced me around into the crowd, and I was this short, runty little nine-year-old, trying to see over the heads of all of these people to figure out where I was.

And then I heard JC screaming: "SERENA! SEREEEENA!"

And people are starting to laugh. And I'm like, "Where are you?" And I start pushing forward . . . and then I find the parade again, and there's JC, in the middle, dancing in a circle, trying to find me. And the parade is going AROUND her, and people are trying to move her back to the side, but no, she's standing RIGHT IN THE MIDDLE of this whole parade, turning in a circle over and over again, yelling, "SERENA! SEREEEEEEEEENA!"

I shoved my way to the crowd, and I ran over to her—SO totally relieved. I thought I was going to be lost in that crowd of tall people for the rest of my life. I was like, "JC!" and I grabbed her hand. And then she grabs my other hand and starts trying to dance like the dancers. We were TERRIBLE—she didn't know the steps any better than I did, but I was just so happy to see her I was like, "Sure, let's dance!" I mean, we couldn't go back to watching the parade like normal people—right? Not after we'd been awesome and part of everything—

This is stupid. I'm not going to cry about something that happened a long time ago. I'm not going to cry.

[deep breath]

Okay! This story is making me really, really sad, so let's wrap it up.

Have you ever had an amazing friend like that? Have you ever BEEN one? Or have you ever danced in a parade—for Memorial Day or any other time? Serena says having a friend like that is the best—and being a friend like that is the bomb. But losing a friend like that . . .

Don't let it happen, right?

[deep breath]

That's my story, and I'm out.

9

Moodopoly

AN HOUR AGO, I had been *so*, so excited to spend the day with JC, just the two of us, for the first time since I'd gotten better. Now, I squeezed my eyes shut, so I wasn't tempted to glare holes in my best friend's head.

The website Mom read says transplant recipients are bored and emotional sometimes during recovery. She said that it's my job to help JC by modeling an attitude that is positive and upbeat. Mom said she read somewhere that transplant patients need *understanding* from friends and family most of all.

Mom hasn't tried playing Monopoly with JC Gerardo, is all I'm saying.

"JC, why are you taking money out of the bank *again*?"

"Uh, *duh*." JC sounded snarky and bored. "You get money when you hit Free Parking."

Now my eyes widened in disbelief. "Uh, no you don't! Free Parking is *not* a thing. Nobody gets money just for hitting a square, unless it's passing Go or somebody lands on their hotel. That's what the rule book says; that's how you play."

Now JC was the one glaring, her face splotched with color. "I wouldn't have gotten it from the bank, except nobody's had to pay taxes. Once we pay taxes, we take it from the middle of the board."

"What?"

JC sighed. "It's only seventy-five dollars, Serena. Jeez."

I threw up my hands. "But that's *NOT* how you play! Taxes go to the BANK like they do IN REAL LIFE. Nobody, like, just gets everyone's tax money because they land on a lucky parking spot."

JC blinked. "Yeah, they do, maybe you've heard of the LOTTERY, Serena? Jeez, I don't even know why I play with you!"

I blew out an angry breath and threw down my top hat. "We don't *have* to play, JC."

JC threw down the rubber duck—the best piece, which she always hogged—and glowered back. "Fine."

"Fine." I exhaled, trying hard to blow out my temper. JC was grumpy sometimes, and she said it was because of her period. But I had my period now—finally!—and I knew not everybody acted mean and snippy during their Lady Days. Sometimes I thought JC just felt like being mean.

I took three deep breaths. I reminded myself that JC probably wasn't feeling good, and that she has been my best friend since the day she asked me to eat lunch with her in the fourth grade, and that best friends forgive each other . . . even when one of them is being completely *ridiculous* and making up rules like she's the High Queen of board games.

After the last breath was blown out, I tried a quieter voice. "So, I'm over Monopoly. What do you want to do now, JC?"

Unfortunately, JC hadn't blown out *her* temper. "I don't know, Serena. Maybe I just want people to come to my house and play a stupid game with me without having a big stupid drama about it."

My jaw dropped, and I sucked in a breath to yell—and remembered. *Best friend. She's my best friend, and she's sick and bored and feels retchy, and best friends forgive each other.* I swallowed hard, choking down my angry words. "Okay. Look, JC, I know—"

"NO, YOU DON'T, SERENA," JC exploded. "You *think* you know. That's your problem."

What? "I—"

"And you *think* you know everything," JC shrilled. "Even though *I'm* the one who gets poked with needles every day, *I'm* the one who has to have blood tests and all of these pills, all the time, for weeks and months and *years*. And *I'm* the one with the headaches and the back pain. *I'm the one* who has to be nice to all the nurses when I'm sick of needles and blood tests or else they'll all think I'm a big baby. You only *think* you know what it's like!"

I felt my shoulders hunching.

Every word JC said felt like she was a balloon blowing up bigger . . . and bigger. The more she yelled, the more room she took up, until there wasn't any room left for me.

Mrs. Gerardo appeared in the doorway and looked at both of us, her forehead wrinkled.

JC kept going, her voice colder and louder. "But *I'm* the one who can't go outside, or my *nanay* freaks and wants to make me wear a mask—even if I'm just walking in the YARD by MYSELF, and it's not like the air is poisonous. *I'm* the one with the pill that makes my stomach *hurt*, and the other stupid pill that makes my hands shake, and—"

"Jolynne," JC's nanay said firmly, pronouncing it like *Jo-leen*. "Take a breath, *anak*. Take a breath."

JC huffed out a breath and glared. Her dark-brown eyes were filled with tears, and, when I looked, her hands were shaking.

"Do you want me to go home?" I said. I was shocked at how shaky my voice was.

"No," snarled JC, but I didn't believe her.

"Jolynne, go get your coat," Mrs. Gerardo said to her daughter. "You have cabin fever again. Your *tatay* will take you girls for a ride." At JC's eye roll, her mother clapped her hands sharply twice. "Go now. You'll feel better, and you'll maybe stop yelling at poor Serena."

"I'm fine," I said, even though rocks were packed tightly in my stomach, and every one of JC's words had punched me where a rock was. Was I acting like a know-it-all? Just because I didn't let JC change the rules to the game? Was I being mean, or was she not being fair?

"It's not fine," Mrs. Gerardo corrected me, "but you're a good girl, Serena."

I didn't *feel* good.

Sometimes, like now, it was exhausting to be JC's best friend.

It was a car full of silent, sulking people that JC's tatay drove down Highway 24 to Fish Ranch Road. Mr. Gerardo took the back roads from there, playing calm music on the stereo. He hummed. We didn't. We didn't talk, or even look at each other. I looked out my window, and JC looked out hers. Lately, we were always looking two different directions. No wonder we couldn't see a way to get along anymore.

Earlier, it had been cloudy, but the sky was clearing a bit, and against the leftover clouds we could see the lights all the way down Wildcat Canyon, and farther out, the Bay, and the lights of the bridge crisscrossing the water. Normally, people drive to the top of Wildcat Canyon to watch the sunset. JC and I always went up there, but afterward, we would drive to Mineral Springs Park to ride the train, or feed the ducks, but of course, JC couldn't. Instead, Mr. Gerardo drove us down the winding roads into the little corner of Noe Avenue where there was a Mitchell's Ice Cream, and he asked us what we wanted.

I ordered a vanilla twirl soft-serve cone.

"Borrrrrrring," JC muttered as she always did. I shrugged, feeling the pinch the word always brought. I was *not* boring. I wasn't! I just liked what I liked. There was nothing wrong with that. There was nothing wrong with *me*.

JC ordered *haluhalo*, which is a Filipino dessert made of a bunch of things: white beans, evaporated milk, shaved ice, coconut, jackfruit, colored gelatin, and caramel flan . . . and a purple yam ice cream called *ube*.

"I've never had beans for dessert." I very carefully did not make a face. *I* wasn't going to yuck her yum.

"They're cooked in sugar," JC defended her choice. "It's good."

The kind of beans in haluhalo were good in lots of things, and jackfruit and flan are really, really sweet. I was sure all the ingredients tasted good . . . separately. I wasn't sure I'd like them together at *all*. White beans *and* purple yam ice cream? No, thank you very much.

Mr. Gerardo got a mix of what JC and I had—vanilla ice cream and ube, with mango . . . and tapioca. *Both* of us made a face at that. While she's getting better, JC's not really supposed to eat sugar very much, but Mr. Gerardo's not supposed to eat *any* sugar.

Mr. Gerardo smiled at us conspiratorially, his round cheeks dimpling as he handed back our yogurt cups at the pickup window. "We don't need to tell Nanay about this, do we, Jojo?"

JC looked at me, rolling her eyes. I smiled at her, a tiny bit.

We stopped at the park down the street to eat. Mr. Gerardo held out his bowl so JC could take a bite of his ice cream, and because it seemed like a polite thing to do, I held out my cone toward Mr. Gerardo. He shook his head and said no thank you.

"What about you, JC? Want a taste?" I offered, holding up the cone.

JC grimaced. Even though she always called my vanilla twirl boring, she'd never actually tasted it. I pulled the cone back with a tight shrug.

"Wait, I want to," JC said quickly. "Just let me use my spoon."

I turned my ice cream so JC could dip her spoon in to a place where my mouth hadn't touched. Her expression as she tasted moved from determined to confused to surprised. "It's pretty good," she said through a mouthful. "Plain vanilla is not as boring as I thought. You should try some of this ube, though."

"Okay," I said. Maybe I would be surprised too.

I tried not to wince as JC scooped a spoonful of bright-purple ice cream onto my cone. I popped it into my mouth, and a super sweet gush of cold creamy flavor flooded my tongue. I swallowed, eyes widening as I nodded. It was *good*. Purple yam ice cream kind of went with vanilla. Who knew?

We dug into our treats in silence, until JC said, "Sooo, about . . . Monopoly . . . Sorry, but we really do get the money from taxes and put it into the Community Chest in the middle."

"Oh. Well . . . sorry, that's not how we play, but not everyone uses the rule book, probably," I said, trying to be fair. "Mom says Fallon and I can't even play anymore, because if Fallon's the banker, she totally cheats."

"Tatay does that too!" JC complained.

"What? Me?" Mr. Gerardo exclaimed, and both of us laughed.

And just like that, our fight was over. JC kept talking as we left the park, pointing out an old car from the fifties with cute taillights, and people with matching Great Danes crossing toward the park. As we were nearly home, JC's phone chirped. She looked at the screen, her face lighting up with a smile.

"Hey, Lani can come over! Tatay, would you mind driving by Lani's house?"

My stomach dropped. We'd been having so much fun, talking and laughing, just like we had before her surgery. Why did JC need someone else right now, when we were having a good time? And she was asking her dad if *he'd* mind her going to Leilani's. What if *I* minded?

"Um, actually, JC," I hesitated, "I can't stay. Mom wanted me to finish my vocabulary homework before she got home. Mr. Gerardo, you can just drop me off at the next block—I can walk from there."

"Don't be ridiculous, Serena," Mr. Gerardo said, meeting my eyes in the front mirror. "Girls who keep up with their homework get dropped off right at the door, like movie stars on a red carpet."

"*Tataaaay,*" JC whined. "Stop making me feel guilty. I'm *going* to do my homework. I just don't feel good right now."

"Probably because you've got an ube sugar rush," I teased.

"Ube makes you do homework faster," JC shot back. "Just wait—I'm gonna be quick like lightning. I'm just choosing my moment, you know?"

"Ha-ha. Right." I climbed out of the car in front

of my house, wishing JC looked even a little sad that I couldn't hang out with her and Leilani all afternoon. "So . . . have fun, I guess."

"Have fun writing out your vocab definitions," JC said, making a disgusted face.

"Yeah, it'll be a party," I joked. "Call me later?"

"Yep," JC promised, eyes already on her phone. "Yay, Lani's brothers are home!"

"Yay," I said, waving as the Gerardos' car pulled off toward Leilani's street. With her eyes bright and her back straight, JC looked better already.

As my eyes took in the difference in the way JC looked, the loneliness that I'd just banished snuck back and curled up behind my ribs again. I wished I'd said something to JC about how much I missed us being us . . . but it seemed like it was already too late.

10

Twin Day Traitor

THE GOOFY MUSIC THAT signaled morning announcements blared from the TV behind Mr. Van's desk on Tuesday morning. I looked up from doodling in my notebook as our class president, Erik Peterson, bellowed, *"Aaaand,* we're live at eight-o-five! Good morning, it's Tuesday. Welcome to morning announcements."

Erik was way, *way* too hyped, and it was only Tuesday.

Today, Erik was reading the announcements wearing a red shirt and suspenders. Because the sixth-grade class officers had declared a monthly Tuesday Twin Day, down the aisle from me, Cameron Jones was wearing the exact same thing, even down to his hair, except his was brown and not blond. He was snickering like a dork every time Erik messed up, and since Erik was blushing and snickering every time he messed up himself, they truly were actually identical idiots right then. It was kind of funny, but kind of not. I was a loner on Twin Day . . . which meant I wasn't exactly showing class spirit. But what was I supposed to do? You can't, like, just twin with someone at the last minute.

At least other people were twinned with kids in 6B, so it didn't look so noticeable that nobody was wearing my exact same outfit.

The eighth-grade girl with Erik—wearing a bright-pink anime wig—wrapped up the announcements with the usual Brigid Ogan script. "And finally, don't forget our motto, Brigid Ogan: Be respectful, be responsible, and be kinder than necessary 'cause you're the bomb. We hope you enjoyed the show. Signing off, I'm Sheila Khoury."

"And I'm Erik Peterson. Thanks for tuning in to Brigid Ogan Middle School morning announcements. Stay classy, Brigid Ogan."

The music came up again, with a montage of today's birthdays, pictures of the student of the week, and various teachers in goofy poses. Harrison's name showed up next to the little dancing cupcake gif, which means that the boy mutant giant is exactly a month and a week older than JC, and ten months older than I am—I don't turn twelve till almost summer.

That reminded me that JC was planning her party already—it was the week before WinterFest, which was seven weeks and two days away. I wondered how her parents were going to make their usual huge party work, when JC had to be careful of germs.

"Happy birthday, Harrison!" Mr. Van told him, and several of my classmates chimed in. I opened my mouth to say something nice—or snarky—to Harrison, but then stopped, breath freezing in my throat.

The last image on the screen after morning announcements is of JC . . . and Leilani Camacho, in JC's bedroom. JC's thick black hair was in a shiny, bouncy side pony, just like Leilani's. Both of them were wearing pink lip gloss, blue overalls, and red T-shirts and caps, like the video game plumber, Mario. Both of them were smiling, and JC held a sign that said, "Happy Twin Day!"

My stomach felt like it was shrinking into a ball

of ice and lightning, burning me from the inside out. For a moment, I couldn't even breathe.

The picture faded, but it felt like it had been burned onto my retinas. It wasn't just their outfits that looked alike—it was everything. JC's smile was wide enough to make her eyes squinch, and show her one dimple, and her braces-bracketed teeth. Her clear brown skin, snub nose, and smiley dark eyes were almost a perfect match for Leilani's. Even their expressions were identical—high cheekbones and rounded cheeks framing that same smug smile. Leilani and JC even had figures—shapes and curves—that my own straight and flat body did not.

Now the burning in my stomach had moved up to my eyes and nose.

Weren't we still friends? Even though JC had hung out with Leilani, why wouldn't she think to 2Face *me* about Twin Day outfits?

She'd taken off the cap, but the overall straps looped over Leilani's shoulders like lanky denim snakes. She and JC must have come up with their twin idea Sunday afternoon . . . after Mr. Gerardo dropped me off at home.

JC and Leilani must have been planning their Twin Day outfits for days—long enough for Leilani to see what JC had in her closet, at least. If I'd gone to Leilani's house, would they have asked me to dress up with them? Could I have been a toad or a princess or something? Or was I so boring that JC would have said that three was too many for Twin Day, and just asked me to hold the camera?

Was JC planning her birthday party with Leilani now?

Mr. Van was standing at the board, writing something down. Around me, everyone else was getting out their notebooks, but I couldn't move.

Mr. Van was opening a window at the front of the classroom when he caught sight of me in my puffy blue coat. "Serena? You're cold? Do you think you're coming down with something again?"

I shook my head. "I'm fine," I said, my voice in almost a whisper. But the truth was, even though it was sunny out, I was freezing. I pulled my coat closer. It felt like I might never get warm again.

SERENA|SAYS

What's up, World? It's Wednesday, and that means *Serena Says* STORYTIME!

So, Twin Day . . . was AWFUL, but Halloween is coming, and hopefully I'll have a better costume moment then. But before Halloween comes Red Ribbon Week, which, like everything else at Brigid Ogan Middle School, is an Event. As the most important person on the Red Ribbon subcommittee, I decided that this year's theme is "Tomorrow, Today."

I came up with that just now, which is as much work as I've done on the whole thing.

So, people—Red Ribbon Week is all about the substance-free life . . . but did I ever tell you that the time I went to the mountains with Bibi and Poppy. Was. Not. Substance. Free? I KNOW, right? Drama!

I was really good at math and reading, so at the end of second grade, my teacher had me doing a lot of extra tests to see if I should skip third grade. While I was testing, my sister's class in fifth grade had a huge puppy party with the sheriff's department drug-sniffer dogs and ice cream, and these Drug-Free T-shirts and stuff. I was super jealous when Fallon told me about it! But then my grandparents came up for a visit, and I mostly forgot about it.

So, on this visit, my bibi wanted to go out to Mt. Veeder, because it's one of those antiquing towns, and they had, like, a quilt show or something. But the real reason we were going was because Poppy, my grandfather, wanted to go to this one brewing company out in the vineyards, because they had some kind of craft root beer, and my poppy is kind of obsessed with root beer.

So, we're ready to go, and Poppy's talking about how he heard they have a vanilla head on the root beer at PJ's. And he's all about how they have notes of cinnamon and maple, and maybe we kids could get some root beer buttons, and he could get himself a barrel? All I heard was "beer."

And I just. Freaked. Out.

One of the things Fallon had told me about her party with the sheriff's department was how NO one should say yes to beer. She'd come home and told us that kids were supposed to "keep it REAL" and Refuse, Explain, Avoid, and Leave when there was beer, and that even going along with the crowd one time could mean that you wouldn't have a good life anymore.

And I was SO sad, because I just loved him so much, but Poppy wasn't going to have a good life because he was going to drink beer—and he was taking Bibi and Fallon and me with him! All the people Mom loved the most! What would happen to us? What should I do?

So we drive to the quilt show, and some antique stores, and finally, it's time for lunch, and Poppy is just READY, you know? He's practically dragging us through the door. And PJ's—it's called a brewing company, but it's a restaurant with wood-fired pizzas and hamburgers and normal stuff, so Fallon, at least, is pretty excited to sit down and order, but I . . . just like BURST out crying, like LOUDLY. Because I see a server coming, and I'm telling Poppy, "You can't drink beer! You can't drink beer!"

And he's like, "What? Bibi? What is the matter with this child?"

DRAMA, okay? It was not cute.

Eventually, Bibi gets us straightened out, and I understood that there's a difference between an ADULT beverage and a root beer, and that root beer buttons are just little candies, and Poppy loves us, and is having a good life, and isn't going to drunk-drive us home or anything. But for a minute there, I was standing up to one of the people I loved the most in the world—scared spitless—but raising my voice and making my stand.

SO! Have you ever felt like you had to stand up for yourself like that? Do you sometimes feel like you

SHOULD stand up for yourself, but you can't figure out what to say? Do your grandparents tell embarrassing stories about you and laugh HARD at you to this day, like mine do??? Do you love craft root beer like my poppy? Serena says you have a voice—so speak out and use it. Even if you're scared to DEATH.

It's kind of dumb—I'm still scared of sharing these vlogs, but I can't call this *Serena Says* if Serena never actually says boo to anyone in real life. So . . . time to start uploading these. Soon.

That's my story, and I'm out.

~ 11 ~

Code Red Ribbons

I STOOD IN THE hallway, book and lunch bag in hand, and blinked.

"What?"

"Student Senate?" Harrison's bristly brows climbed. "We had an assignment? For Red Ribbon Week? Our substance-free awareness thing? Hello?" He reached out with a fist to knock on my forehead, but I twisted out of reach.

"Crud, crud, cruddy, crud," I muttered, and bent to slide my book down the side pocket of my rolling backpack. Other than my imaginary theme, after seeing JC's picture during morning announcements Tuesday, I'd pretty much forgotten all about the stupid senate thing. A subcommittee. I was on a subcommittee with Boy Mutant. Whee.

"Fine, I'm coming," I said tiredly. "What are we supposed to do?"

"Make sure you have your notebook," Harrison said, still breathing down my neck. "Mrs. Henry likes us to take notes."

"Of *course* she does," I muttered, zipping my bag and dragging it down the hall behind me.

Harrison followed as I stomped down the hall. "Do you have any great ideas?"

Great ideas? *Please.* I scowled down at the tiles. "What's the point?"

"What's the point of what?" Harrison demanded. "Ideas? Red Ribbon Week? Keeping people off drugs?"

When I didn't answer, Harrison made a frustrated noise. "Are you going to be a lame partner?"

I was grinding my teeth. "I'm not lame. I know people shouldn't do drugs," I grumped, digging in my bag for my lunchtime snacks. "Some drugs are legal, though."

"Not all of them. And anyway, what's legal is *not* the point," Harrison lectured. "The point is that drugs destroy lives. The point is that kids are just starting their lives. The point is—"

"I *know* what the point is, Harrison. Jeez Louise."

"Whatever." Harrison's shoulders slumped on a big sigh. "When Mrs. Henry asks for our ideas, I'll start. If you think of anything, you can add it at the end. Okay?"

I stiffened. *If* I thought of anything? "Why are *you* first? How do you know I don't have a whole list of things I thought of already?"

Harrison rolled his eyes. "Because you didn't even remember you were *on* senate, that's how." Shaking his head, Harrison lengthened his stride, leaving me behind. "Keep up, Hobbit."

"Shut it, Mutant."

Mrs. Bowers smiled as we walked through the administration office; me, glowering and out of breath, Harrison, just beyond reach of my kick. Harrison continued straight through to Mrs. Henry's open door. I took a moment to open my notebook and scrawl furiously before shoving my pen in my pocket and following. I did *too* have ideas.

There was an upholstered loveseat in Mrs. Henry's office where Sunita and Ally were already sitting, with Eliana, who was our class treasurer as well as our Student Senate representative, parked beside them in her chair. The rest of the seats were folding chairs, organized into a half circle around the front of Mrs. Henry's desk. She sat behind it, her gold-rimmed half glasses sliding down her nose, while she typed something into her notepad. Ignoring the seat next to Harrison, I dragged a chair next to Eliana. In a few minutes, Sunita called the meeting to order and we got started.

Eliana gave us a report on the amended Winter-Fest budget, which we voted to accept. I scowled. The word "WinterFest" was in all caps on top of Eliana's paper, and with the countdown at six weeks, I wasn't ready. Six weeks! I didn't want to think about it. I hadn't even picked a project, much less bought the supplies or started work. How was I ever going to pull all this together?

Cameron droned on about turnouts for basketball, announcing that they were organizing a canned food drive for Thanksgiving. Hyung reported on plans for a service project for winter quarter. Through most of the unexciting meeting, Mrs. Henry looked like she was working on something else. She wasn't even eating. I wasn't paying attention really either—I was rolling my tangerine peels, wishing that instead of waiting for JC to call, that I'd called her about the Twin Day thing. I wondered if it was too late.

Suddenly, Sunita looked from me to Harrison. "If the Red Ribbon subcommittee is ready with their report . . . ," she began.

I choked on the piece of tangerine in my mouth as Mrs. Henry looked up from her computer and smiled—evilly, probably. *No*, I was *not* ready, but Harrison jumped to his feet. He swung his briefcase onto the seat behind him and popped open the clasps.

"We're ready," he said, pulling out a thick sheaf of papers.

I rolled my eyes, but privately, I was a teeny-tiny bit impressed. Harrison had a whole pile of notes. He looked like a teacher, getting ready to hand out worksheets. To my horror, he handed the stack of paper to Sunita and said, "Take one and pass it on, please," just like Mr. Van always said. I stifled a groan as I looked down at the title on the top sheet. THE HISTORY OF RED RIBBON WEEK was in all caps and centered.

I wasn't the only one slumping. Mrs. Henry cleared her throat. "Remember, Harrison," she said, "we only have forty-five minutes for lunch."

"I know," Harrison muttered, the tips of his ears turning pink where they stuck out from his shaggy brown curls. "It's just my research. I'm not going to read it or anything."

Eliana gave a choked cough that sounded a lot like a belly laugh stuffed down. I was caught between feeling embarrassed for Harrison and feeling annoyed. This was supposed to be *our* subcommittee, not Harrison's personal committee of one. If he'd told me he was going to do this, I would have told him no. Then everyone wouldn't be laughing at him.

"I thought some of you might like to know the history of Red Ribbon Week," Harrison said determinedly, waving to the paper, "and why we even *do* this every year. I, um"—Harrison ducked his head awkwardly—"well, I hope you read it. I hope it helps you understand why I—I mean, our subcommittee— decided to do Red Ribbon Week with some Career Day stuff."

Career Day? He couldn't have given me a hint about this on the way to the meeting?

Looking through the handout was actually interesting—Harrison found the story of Red Ribbon Week and put in all this stuff about when it became an official week in schools, a long time ago. But it didn't have anything to do with Brigid Ogan . . . at all.

"We can have people wear red, and all the rest of that, like we usually do, but I just thought this would be better." Harrison gestured to the paper again. "I mean, just read it, and you'll know what I mean."

Having Career Day stuff for the last day was kind of good, though. I could feel ideas sparking through my head. We could do some *fun* things with this. I know JC's mom—

I stopped that thought cold. JC wasn't going to be someone I would be talking to about this. Not anymore.

Right?

"Well, Harrison, this is good," Sunita was saying cautiously. "But you don't have, like, activities lined up?"

The silence that followed was excruciating. Harrison shifted from foot to foot, the pink from the tips of his ears migrating across his cheeks and neck. He cleared his throat. "Um. Uh, well, I, I mean—"

We *could* have had fun with this—JC and me—but now, I'd have to do this myself.

"He means no, he doesn't," I blurted. "I mean, Harrison doesn't. Yet. That's my part. The activities, I mean."

Eliana, who'd been watching me scribble in my notebook, turned wide eyes toward me. And Harrison, who had absolutely no chill, gave me a horrified look.

"Serena?" His loud whisper was completely audible in the quiet room, "What are you doing?"

Mrs. Henry took off her glasses, the smile broad across her sharp-chinned face. "Now *this* sounds like the kind of teamwork that I like. Serena St. John, let's hear from you."

Uh-oh.

I stood up slowly, stopping to pull up my socks so I could stall. The pressure of so many eyes on me felt like tiny weights against my body. I cleared my throat and looked at the big flower pin on Mrs. Henry's shoulder instead of directly at her face, so I could avoid her sharp eyes.

"Harrison, um, had a lot of good ideas about Career Day, and since Red Ribbon Week is so close to Halloween, I thought we could, um, decorate? Like, have a Deck the Doors contest on Monday, you know, to decorate our homeroom doors with an anti-drug theme?"

I could hear my voice rising at the end of every line, as if I were asking a question. Mom always asked me if I was asking her or telling her something when I did that. I cleared my throat again, trying to sound sure of what I was saying. "And then on Tuesday, we can have a College Day maybe? So people can wear logo clothes from schools and colleges and stuff? And Wednesday," I looked down at the scribbles in my notebook, "is Dreams Before Drugs, which is basically pajama day, which will be really easy."

I snuck a glance at Ally, who gave me a thumbs-up. My mouth curved into a tiny grin.

"Um, Thursday, it's Free to Plan a Future, and people can dress up like their future jobs. And Friday at assembly, we can have a Red Ribbon Rally and hand out awards for the door contest, and um, I was thinking, parents came to our class for a career fair when we were in elementary, and—"

"Oh! A career fair!" Sunita interrupted. "Good idea! We could have tables and booths in the cafeteria at lunch on Friday!"

"Uh, we need a fundraiser if we're going to have prizes," Eliana pointed out. "I mean, we have money in the budget, but we should do something . . . or sell something."

"Can we sell candy?" Hyung wanted to know. "I

don't think basketball is doing candy bars this year, are they, Cam?"

Little conversations popped up around the room, as the whole senate started brainstorming. Sunita called for an official vote to accept our ideas, and when it passed, I dropped back into my seat, breathing a sigh of relief.

I leaned over to look at Harrison, who still looked a little rattled, and gave him a smug smile. "Who knew? I had more than one great idea!"

Harrison rolled his eyes. He leaned forward, voice low. "Hobbit, you do realize that we have to *do* all the stuff you just came up with, right?"

"What? No, we're just idea people," I argued, feeling my stomach sink. He couldn't be serious, could he? The dress-up days wouldn't be a big deal, but the prizes and the judging and the Career Day would be a lot of work.

"Idea people? Wanna bet?" Harrison laughed.

In a few minutes, Sunita tapped her gavel and wrapped up the meeting. "Thanks to our subcommittee, we have a ton of ideas and a lot of directions to go. Hyung and Cameron, if you could follow up on the candy sales, that would be great. Ally, if you could get something to the morning announcements team, that would help. Serena and Harrison, let us know what you need to get that career fair going."

"I'm excited to work with you both," Mrs. Henry chimed in, beaming at us.

Great, I thought, giving her a weak smile. *Just great.*

12

Nosy St. John

"SOOO, THERE'S A BOY downstairs?" Fallon, brows raised, stood sock-footed in my doorway late Saturday afternoon, staring while she wound her box braids into a knot on the top of her head.

"Yeah?" I dumped my backpack on my bed and rooted around for my gel pens. Navy, bronze, red, green, and . . . aha, the black one. I surveyed the mess of wadded paper napkins, gum wrappers, hair bands, torn pieces of binder paper, and bent notebooks and decided I'd reload my bag later. I had plenty of time before Monday morning.

"And he's . . . a friend of yours?"

"He is?" I frowned over at my sister. "Is that what he said?"

She nodded, brows raised.

"Dang it, Mutant," I mumbled, and dug through the mess on my bed for my Red Ribbon binder. Harrison was the good kind of organized, once he got started, but he didn't seem to understand that working together didn't mean talking every day. He'd called me twice since Wednesday to nitpick things, and it was totally just like him to show up at my house to nitpick some more.

"Well?" Fallon demanded as I moved toward the door, binder in hand. "Do you know who it is? Do you *like* him? Aren't you going to try to do"—she gestured vaguely at my hair, which was in relaxed weekend mode—"something with that?"

I closed my door halfway to assess myself in the mirror behind it. Gray sweatpants and navy hoodie, check. Fleece beanie with curls sticking out around back and sides, check. Red Ribbon stuff, check. "Yep, nope, and heck no," I told my sister, deciding I looked fine. "It's just Harrison."

"That's not Harrison," Fallon insisted, trailing me down the stairs. "I remember that guy from your fifth-grade class. This guy isn't just big, he's really, *really* tall."

"He grew," I said, ducking through the hallway

into the kitchen. By now I recognized Harrison's voice. Come to think of it, he *had* been bigger around before he'd gotten bigger up-and-down last summer. Huh.

In the kitchen, I raided Mom's stash of salted caramel and chocolate lollipops. Since Harrison was company, I was sure I'd be allowed to have them in the front room. I pulled out a few extra for Harrison to choose between, then headed back.

Fallon was still in the hallway, peeking around the corner into the front room. As I passed her, she snatched off my beanie and picked at my hair with nimble fingers. "Fallon," I whined, exasperated as she fluffed and tucked, this time leaving a pouf of curls exposed in the front half of my head, while the rest was covered.

"It feels weird like that," I complained, reaching to adjust my hat again, but my sister swatted my hands away.

"It looks cute like that. Leave it," she instructed.

Fallon was bossy most of the time, but not usually about my style. I decided to take her advice this time. "Thanks. Can I go now, Mommy?"

Fallon rolled her eyes and waved me on.

I walked around the corner, making a course

correction when I saw my mother was in the papasan chair across from where Harrison was seated on the couch. I headed toward the corner of the sectional opposite him and plopped down, tossing the lollipops on the couch cushion between us. "Hey. Want one?"

"Hey. Um, sorry to barge in." Harrison, for once, wasn't wearing plaid, but a pale-blue button-up shirt and a cardigan sweater, like one of Mr. Van's. He looked weirdly old dressed up, his big fingers gripping that stupid briefcase. I could see that he'd bitten his thumbnail down to where it was pink and gross. "Mom and Dad had, um, something to do, so I had them drop me off. If you have a second, we need to look at a few more things—"

I sighed loudly. Harrison was obsessed—and stubborn, and he had a tack in his tushie about anything to do with this Red Ribbon Week. "Couldn't we do this tomorrow?" I groaned.

My mother drew breath, but I didn't wait for her to correct my attitude. "I didn't mean that, I apologize," I mumbled ungraciously. "What is it now?"

As Harrison opened up his briefcase and wrestled out a fat folder, Mom got up, saying something about making us some sandwiches, and bustled into the kitchen.

I watched her go, turning suspicious eyes on Harrison. "Dude, what did you *do*?"

Harrison looked confused. "What, to your mom? Nothing."

"Well, you must have done something. First off, we *never* get to eat stuff with crumbs in the front room. Ever. Second, she always says if our friends want something to eat, we know where the kitchen is. She does *not* make sandwiches." I tilted my head and studied him. "Whatever you did, it worked. You're like the Parent Whisperer. Gold star, Mutant." I grinned.

Harrison opened his mouth, closed it, and frowned. His nostrils flared as he exhaled.

I spoke around the lollipop shoved in between my back teeth. "What?"

"I didn't do anything. She probably just feels sorry for me," Harrison said, opening his notebook. "Okay. I thought if we had them set up the tables across the back—"

"Wait, what?" I interrupted. "Feels sorry for you why? What's wrong with you?"

Harrison sighed. "Nothing. I just told her my parents are at New Vista."

I gasped, leaning back in my seat in shock, then

gulped and hastily smoothed my expression. I tried to play it off like I'd just sneezed, but I wasn't fooling anyone.

Mom worked as an advanced practice psychiatric nurse at New Vista, so I knew it was a hospital for people with serious mental problems. I also knew that making the face I'd just made or asking any of the nosy questions I wanted to would be rude enough for Mom to do more than suck in a breath to correct me.

"Um," I flailed, searching for words. "Your *parents*—? You— I— Never mind. Sorry."

Harrison gave me a sickly smile. "And now you feel sorry for me too."

"No! No, I don't, Mutant," I said quickly. "For all I know, your parents are doctors."

Harrison heaved a sigh and picked his cuticle. "Well, Mom *is* a doctor. But she's an endocrinologist." Harrison shrugged. "They're just visiting my brother today, like they always do after church."

I sank my teeth into my bottom lip, hoping the pinch of pain would remind me not to be too curious. "I didn't know you had a brother."

"Well . . . he's a lot older," Harrison explained, watching me carefully. "Six years."

"Oh. My sister's older too." I opened my mouth again, but then bit down on my lip, hard—*no more questions, Serena*—and opened my binder. *I will not be nosy. I will not be nosy. I will not* . . . "Okay, so what's this about tables in the back?"

Harrison closed his binder with a heavy sigh. "You want to know about my brother, don't you? Just ask."

Duh, was he *serious*? Of course I did! I opened my mouth . . . then chickened out.

"Nope, it's fine, Harrison, I don't want to know." The lie shoved its way out of my mouth. "Now—are you rearranging where you're putting the parent volunteers? What's the new plan now?"

It's probably better that I didn't ask. I mean, I didn't know what to say, so I did the right thing to stop talking about it, right? Even though I maybe hurt Harrison's feelings . . .

Why doesn't doing the right thing feel right?

⌒ 13 ⌒

A Word Is Dead (When It Is Said)

"HEY, REE." JC'S VOICE was distracted. I'd tried to 2Face her like I always did after school, but she said I should call so I knew she was doing something else, probably painting her nails.

"So, hey," I said, trying to sound bright and interesting. Since I'd waited for her call, we hadn't talked since our Monopoly date. "So, I made another couple of vlogs. I'm getting better at it—kind of. I haven't uploaded any of them yet, but think I'm going to try for reporter again next semester, definitely. Maybe."

"Uh-huh," JC said.

I cleared my throat. "Yeah, so that's what I'm doing. What's going on with you?"

"Just hanging out," JC said. "I'm watching some-thing."

Oh. JC was probably watching that stupid *Modern Divas* again. I would have asked Mom if we could have subscription TV so I could watch it, too, but Fallon said Mom had already told *her* no. Fallon just goes to Sharyn's house to watch it.

"So tomorrow is Red Ribbon Week," I blurted.

"Yep," JC yawned. "Same as last year."

"No, better than last year. It's going to be good. *I'm* organizing it," I argued. "Student Senate is work-ing hard."

"Huh," JC said. I couldn't tell if her voice was thoughtful or if she was being sarcastic. "I thought you said senate was stupid."

I fidgeted. I should have known JC would remem-ber how I'd gone on about senate when Fallon was on it. "It kind of is, but it's kind of not," I said finally. "I mean, Harrison is *way* too into it, and everyone knows Mrs. Henry's the one deciding things, but she's letting us do new stuff for Red Ribbon Week."

I cleared my throat. JC didn't say anything.

"And, um, Thursday, it's Free to Plan a Future, and we're dressing up like our future jobs. And Friday at the Red Ribbon Rally, we're handing out awards for a door contest, and there's a career fair at lunch, and parent volunteers are coming. . . . At the next senate meeting, Eliana's collecting money from the classes selling red candy in the cafeteria. We're donating it to this place called Liberation Library. It's books for kids in juvenile detention centers."

I paused again. I couldn't hear . . . anything. Had JC put down the phone? She did that sometimes, when her mom called her after school.

"JC?"

"Uh-huh, cool," JC said a moment later.

My face burned. Couldn't she put her show on pause for five minutes? She hadn't even texted me for days. "So should I call you later, JC, or what?"

"No! No, I'm listening," JC said, but she wasn't. I knew she wasn't. She was watching her divas, and all I was doing was interrupting.

Why was I still trying?

"Hey, JC, did you know Harrison Ballard's brother is at New Vista?" I said the words in a whispered rush, my stomach swooping sickeningly as I blurted the words. I wanted to take them back immediately.

There was a pause, and I hoped, I *prayed* that she hadn't heard me. Then a second later, JC gasped.

"Wait, what? Did you say that Harrison Ballard's

brother is a psycho? Really?"

I winced. At our house, the word "crazy" is worse than a swear. Mom says it's a term people use when they're too lazy to do the hard work of understanding and empathy. She gets angry when people call New Vista a "loony bin" too. "Don't say that. And don't tell anyone, either, okay?" I begged. "He's sick, but he's getting better." I had no idea if that was true, but it sounded like it could be.

"OMG," JC whispered back. "Did you find out from your mom?"

"What? No!" I exclaimed in my normal voice. "JC, you *know* Mom would never, ever tell me about her patients' private business. She wouldn't even tell me if *you* were at New Vista."

She wouldn't either. And if she found out that I'd been the one telling . . . I winced again.

"Whatever, just asking," JC said. Her face was so close to the phone now, I could hear her crunching on something—probably dry ramen noodles, which JC always ate when she was watching TV. "You know, I didn't even remember Harrison *had* a brother. He ran away or something a long time ago. . . . Wow, he must have been at New Vista forever. How'd you find out?"

"Uh, I just heard it around," I said, suddenly

reluctant to tell JC that Harrison had told me. I didn't want to think about Harrison at all right then.

"Well, if it's true . . . that is really sad," JC said, her voice serious. "I wonder if that's why Harrison's into Red Ribbon Week. Maybe his brother did drugs, and that's how he got put at New Vista."

I swallowed, queasy. What if that were true? "I don't know anything more. Harrison probably doesn't want us to feel sorry for him. Anyway, his brother's, like, eighteen, so he's way older."

"Way, way older than you," JC said, reminding me that I was the youngest in our class. "You should do something for him," JC continued. "Something nice."

"For Harrison's brother?" I blurted.

"For Harrison," JC said, as if this were obvious. "You know he likes you."

"Would you stop? He does not! And, anyway, I'm already nice," I said, my voice sharp. "Don't make this weird, JC."

"It's not that big a deal to do something nice for someone, Serena," JC said, sounding snippy. "You should try it sometime."

"JC, I'm *nice*!" Now I sounded angry. "I do nice things all the time."

JC gusted out a sigh. "Serena, you know what

I mean. Look, I'll just ask Lani if she can think of something for our class to do for him. She's good at that."

It felt like the floor dropped out from underneath me. "What? NO! Don't tell Leilani!" I gasped. "JC, you promised!"

"No, I didn't. Anyway, you said, 'Don't tell anyone.' Leilani is not just anyone," JC pointed out with a debater's logic. "She's the class ambassador. This is the kind of thing ambassadors should know, Ree, so they can do outreach and stuff. What if no one knew that I was going to the hospital, huh? No one would have visited me."

"But—"

"Jeez, Serena, I'm not going to tell the whole world. I just think our class should do something for his family—like, anonymously. Don't you remember the Brigid Ogan motto? We're supposed to be kinder than necessary."

"I know, but—"

"We'll think of something *super* good—maybe make it a class project. I'll talk to Lani and see what she says." JC's voice warmed. "You know Lani always has the *best* ideas. No offense, Ree. You were an okay ambassador, but Leilani is *amazing*."

I flinched. Amazing? Leilani was amazing, and I was only *okay*?

"And she'll come up with something everyone will be into. This is going to be great—it's going to be epic, Serena. Trust me."

The word "trust" made me flinch again. I couldn't trust myself right now—I didn't know what I was doing anymore. Trust seemed like something fragile and good, something I couldn't be allowed to hold on to anymore.

All I could think of was the way Harrison had looked at me when he'd said, "Just ask," as if he'd been kind of . . . challenging me? Maybe asking me because he *wanted* to talk about his brother? Something about the hunch of his shoulders and the way his chin tipped down had made me a little afraid. He said he'd tell me anything I wanted to know, but suddenly it had all felt like too much—and too weird. I lied—and Harrison hadn't looked at me again. Just pulled out his big stupid binder, and our subcommittee of two had gone on with more of his Boy Mutant nitpicking.

How could I trust JC after she'd said she was going to tell Leilani everything? No way. I'd messed up big-time, and all I could trust now was that this was going to be a total *disaster*.

SERENA|SAYS

What's up, World? It's Wednesday, and Serena says . . . it's STORYTIME.

Welcome back to my vlog!

So this story is about a girl that we'll call . . . um, Leah, to protect the not-so-innocent. This is about the first time I met her at my middle school.

[deep breath]

So our cafeteria at school is actually amazing. I know, I know, school cafeteria food is supposed to be super nasty, but ours isn't, right? So anyway, it was Taco Thursday, and I saw this girl in line in front of me, telling the cafeteria lady not to put cheese on her taco, right? And I didn't think much about it—people eat whatever, right? But the reason why I noticed her was that she was wearing this really cute sweatshirt and skirt—kind of a ruffled prairie thing or whatever, and I remember thinking her boots went with it really well.

SO ANYWAY. She'd asked for no cheese, and then we ended up at the drink fridge together, and she was getting one of these drinks that's some kind of fruit flavor, and either yogurt or some sports drink stuff in it. And I look at her tray, and she's taken one of the yogurt drink ones. So I said, "You know that has milk in it, right?"

Because she'd just said she didn't want cheese, right? So I was—I mean, I don't know, maybe she just didn't like cheese, but I just thought she should know there was milk in something, like if she was vegan, right? Or what if she was lactose intolerant? Wouldn't she want to help a girl out, if she was in my shoes? But no.

She gives me this "duh" face, and she's like, "Yeah, I know it has milk in it, it's A YOGURT DRINK." And she stares at me like I just spit on her tray or something.

And I felt so stupid I didn't even explain. I was like, "Um, yeah, okay, bye."

Gah, awkward, right? I hate even remembering this whole conversation.

Ugh, not that I'm going to upload this, but if it was YOUR first day at a school, would you come for people like that? Or would you maybe try and be really chill and make friends? Is it more important to tell people you know something to look smart? Or is it more important that people think you're nice?

The thing is, not everyone always makes a good first impression . . . I DEFINITELY didn't with Leilani . . . I mean, Leah. And, okay, so she made a REALLY bad first impression on me, and I didn't even try to like her after that, which . . . okay, so that's not really fair, even though she was RUDE. I know, I know—I should've given her a chance. People change, all the time. Just look at JC . . . and me . . .

[pause]

Um . . . okay, so Serena says being chill with new people is where it's at and giving people a chance is a superpower. It's important to be a friend—a REAL friend—whenever you can.

That's my story, and I'm out.

14

Sixth Grade Is Not Forever

FOR DINNER, WE HAD Goop Over Rice, a "fast food" Mom invented for when she'd run out of time to do more than run the rice steamer and add leftovers. It was Fallon's turn to help, so I was still deep in my thoughts by the time Mom called me to eat.

I'd wanted a nap and a chance to figure things out, just in case I talked to Harrison, but one look at my backpack convinced me there wasn't time. Sixth graders in Mr. Howard's language arts class at Brigid Ogan have more homework projects than anyone. Language arts worksheets were the *worst*, filled with words no one ever used to describe things so obvious they made me want to scream.

I rested my chin on my hand and moodily stirred the mixture of rice, corn, beans, peppers, cheese, and chopped sausage on my plate, almost too tired to eat . . . and cranky with Mr. Howard, Harrison, JC—everyone.

"Serena?"

I mean, seriously. Why had Leilani decided to take over my job as class ambassador? Why did she always have to show everyone that she was better than me at everything?

"SERENA."

And what if Harrison listened to JC and Leilani? We didn't have room to add any new awards at Brigid Ogan—not even if JC and Leilani did all the work themselves, which Leilani might, since that's kind of how she rolled. And what about all the work Harrison and I—

"Serena St. John. Earth to Serena, come in, please."

"Huh?" I blinked at my mother's skeptical expression. "What?"

My mother gave me a mommish look, the kind that examines faces and body language for secrets that only mothers can interpret. I met her eyes, looking as normal as I could, but still she studied me, a frown rumpling the smooth brown expanse of her forehead.

"Where's your head tonight, Rena-Beana-Belle? What's going on with you?"

I ducked away from the all-seeing eyes. "Nowhere. Nothing."

Mom pinched the bridge of her nose and looked up, addressing the ceiling. "First 'nowhere,' now 'nothing.' How did I know that's what she was going to try to tell me, God?"

The phone rang, and I jumped. My mother gave me another look, frowning again. I felt silly when I realized it was her cell phone, with the special ring that meant New Vista.

She paused a moment before swiping the screen, coming around the table, and laying her hand on my forehead. "Serena mine, are you coming down with something again?"

"No," I said, ducking away from her touch. "Answer your phone."

Mom answered it, giving me a narrow-eyed look. "Nova St. John. Yes, Kathy, hello."

No one at our house—or even at Bibi and Poppy's house—is allowed on the phone at the table, but when Mom's on call at the hospital, the rules are different for her. After a moment, as Mom moved away from the table and into the hallway for privacy, Fallon took advantage of Mom's absence to pull out her phone. Her thumbs moved busily.

"She's going to take your phone again," I predicted as a muted chime indicated an incoming text.

"Mind your own biscuits," Fallon said, reading greedily.

I shrugged. Both of us listened with half an ear to Mom's work voice, which sounded professional and calm. She was frowning when she came back to the table, though, which meant she probably had to go back to the hospital to fix something. Her frown deepened on seeing my sister's phone.

"Fallon Celeste—" She pointed an accusing finger at the offending object.

Fallon shoved her phone out of sight while radiating an expression of intense innocence.

Sighing, my mother turned to me. "Here's the thing, Rena-Beana. I don't have time to wait for you to decide to talk. It's been a long day, I've got to go back in tonight, and you've probably still got homework. I can't help if I don't know what's going on, so speak now, kiddo." She picked up her fork. "The clock is ticking."

I slumped. Sometimes, I wish I had a movie mom, one who came to my room for long, private talks and brought cupcakes. I licked my lips, trying to think of how to begin.

Across the table, Fallon suddenly straightened. "Is this about *Har*-ri-son?" she asked, drawing out his name in syrupy tones.

I flinched. How did she—

"Are you for real? This is about a *boy*? Oh-em-gee," Fallon squealed. "Our little Rena Jelly Beana's growing up now!"

"Shut up, Fallon. *Mom!*" I complained, hoping for rescue. "Make her stop!"

"Re*na*," my mother mimicked in perfect imitation. "Words without whining, please; I've already got a headache. Fallon, stop baiting your sister," she added as Fallon batted her eyes and made a big show of closing an imaginary zipper across her mouth.

"It's not about Harrison like that," I mumbled, shooting daggers at my sister. "I . . . he . . ."

"Oh, jeez." Fallon groaned, her vow of silence forgotten. "What did you do now?"

"Shut up! Nothing! I—" The lie stuck, a sharp twinge digging in my throat.

Fallon rolled her eyes. "Would you spit it out? You always get all worked up about whatever, and then it's nothing. Whatever it is, Serena, Harrison probably hasn't even noticed."

"Fallon St. John, that is *enough*." Mom's warning was the kind that meant business.

A fierce ache started up in the corners of my eyes. I pinched my nose to steady myself. Maybe it *was* nothing. Harrison hadn't said anything about talking to JC or Leilani. Mr. Van had patted my shoulder and told me that he'd known I'd do a great job.

It wasn't true, though. I knew exactly what kind of job I'd done.

"It's . . . nothing," I said, voice wobbling.

"It doesn't look like nothing from here, Rena-Bean." My mother's hand landed on my back, tapping softly. "Are you sure you don't need to talk?"

"Yeah." She would be so disappointed if she knew. I decided to tell my mother one truth, if not all of them. "I just . . . JC said some stuff, and we had an argument. It's stupid but," I swallowed the gravel in my throat, "I haven't heard anything about her birthday party. I'm probably not invited. We're . . . not really friends anymore."

The weight of Mom's hand against my shoulder blades anchored me as I blinked back sudden tears. When JC came back to school, everything was going to be different. I'd not been besties with anyone else for so long; I didn't know how, or where, to start. Sometimes I wished I were seven again, and all I had to do was go and sit on Mom's lap, and everything got fixed. But sixth grade wasn't like second—and there was no lap in the world that would make JC like me as much as she had before.

And that was sad enough to make my heart pinch. A sob erupted from my chest, surprising me.

"Oh, Serena," Mom sympathized, squeezing my shoulder as I sniffled. "I'm sorry growing up is so hard. Friend stuff can be tricky at this age, but you'll figure it out. It gets better. I promise, sixth grade is not forever."

"Truth," Fallon seconded glumly from her side of the table. "It only feels like it. Getting to seventh takes till eternity. It lasts forever, and then eighth . . ."

Mom made an exasperated noise. "Fallon! I am trying to make your sister feel *better*, not *worse*."

"Well, I'm sorry, but this girl's got to keep it real," Fallon argued.

Through the tears, a snorty laugh burst out. At least one thing would never change. The world might be ending, but my sister Fallon was still the same giant pain in the butt.

SERENA|SAYS

What's up, World? It's your girl Serena, and I'm . . . yeah. Not great.

Today, I'm telling my own story, so it's going to get kind of REAL, because I have a LOT going on and I have to practice how I'm going to say it. Basically, school stuff and friend stuff and friends-at-school stuff, you know the drill. But first, a question for my loyal viewers—okay, the IMAGINARY loyal viewers who will be super loyal when I start uploading these someday—if you tell someone a secret that everyone already knows, is it still . . . telling?

You know, people gossip and tell stories to each other all the time. And I always try to, like, use good judgment and think when I tell a story. I ask myself, what if, like, my bestie told one of my secrets? Like, what if she told people that I was afraid of big dogs, or still had to sleep with a night-light, or . . . what if she told everyone I'd wet my bed till I was seven? Even though—probably—nobody cares, people would still laugh, and I would still DIE, right? Because friends don't tell stories that aren't ours to tell, right? It's about . . . keeping your word. Or, really, kind of like keeping the unspoken promises between friends, that you've got their back, and they've got yours.

So.

Today's story is . . . about a time I DIDN'T do that.

[pause]

So I told someone something I thought was interesting—but it was a secret someone else had told me, so it totally wasn't my secret to tell. At all. And I knew that.

Sometimes, you just KNOW that someone is telling you something that they haven't told everyone—and you know that person is taking a huge chance and trusting you, even if they haven't said it's a secret. This person trusted me, and . . . I wish I hadn't tried so hard to say something interesting that I said something stupid.

I think I feel the worst about the other person.

It's so stupid. He's loud, and he always leans on me and bangs into me with that briefcase. AND when I got my hair relaxed in fourth grade for pictures, and Mom curled it under, he said my hair looked like a mushroom, and he called me Toadstool all day. He's not even nice! We're not even friends, but I . . . I don't want him to think . . .

He just looked so . . . balled up when he was talking to me. Like when your stomach hurts, you know, and you hunch over? That's how he looked. I—

[looks off to the side of screen]

Oh, retch.

That's my phone. I still don't know what to say! And now, I'm out of time.

[looks off to the side of the screen, reaches forward to turn off camera]

15

Sorry Is the Hardest Word

"AND SHE TOLD YOU everybody knows?" Harrison's voice through the phone is quiet.

"Right." I wiped my sweaty hands on my pants and clutched the phone tighter to my ear. The flat rectangle of the receiver suddenly fit awkwardly in my hand. "Um, so, I just wanted to say—"

"They probably do. Know, I mean," Harrison said, slowly, like he was mulling it over. "Still, it was kind of a lame thing to do. If I'd wanted everyone to talk about how my brother was at New Vista, I would have told them, so thanks for that. I wouldn't have told *you*, except . . . I wanted to. But you freaked out and all, so I didn't."

"Wait, what? I didn't freak. I—"

"I just mean, you obviously didn't want to know. You changed the subject," Harrison continued, his voice tight. "That's—whatever, I guess. It isn't catching, just for the record."

"What? What isn't? What are you talking about?"

"You know what I'm talking about. Just because Lance has mental problems doesn't mean you're going to catch them from me. I'm just saying."

Even through the phone, the tired anger in his voice made me embarrassed and ashamed. I couldn't find words fast enough to tell him he was wrong. "Harrison, that's—I never—"

"So, *anyway*," Harrison said loudly, clearly the one changing the subject now, "I talked to Leilani about an idea she had for a new Senate award. She wants people to vote for a person they know has had a hard time but has stayed positive. She wants to award them a Brigid Ogan Buoyancy Award. And maybe a medal with a balloon on it or something, because they're 'staying up,' which is kind of silly, but whatever."

I bit my lip. That wasn't the whole reason for the award, and I knew it.

Harrison sighed. "It wouldn't hurt, you know,

saying that stuff sometimes is hard."

"I know stuff is sometimes hard," I said, "but that's part of what I'm trying to tell you. Leilani and JC only thought up the award so they could give an award to you. I thought you'd care!"

"Senators aren't eligible," Harrison said impatiently. "We're never eligible for awards from programs we organize, you should know that. So do we do it, or what? Do you still have a problem with it? To me, it doesn't have anything to do with substance abuse, but if we move it to WinterFest, when we give out class awards, that's fine with me."

"I—no. Fine. Okay. Whatever." I was done fighting.

"Fine. I'll figure it out with Lani."

Not again. I scowled. "Harrison, I'm on this subcommittee too. Do you want me to—"

"No," Harrison said loudly. "I don't need you."

"Fine." I sighed, feeling bruised. "I'm sorry, Harrison. And . . . I'm sorry about your brother, okay? . . . Harrison? Hello?"

You can look at a phone's screen and tell when a call drops, but my phone is Mom's old one, so it only shows the caller's name and number and a tiny counter, counting up the minutes of the call. When

I took it from my ear, it held only Harrison's name and number, and nothing more.

He was gone and hadn't even said goodbye.

After a brief knock, the door to my room burst open.

I recognized my sister's pushy entrance. If Mom had knocked and I hadn't answered, *she* would have left me alone, but Fallon leaned over me where I lay curled under my covers and poked my shoulder.

"Hey. I know you're awake," she said, turning up my night-light.

I rolled onto my side to face her. "What?"

I'd tried to cry myself to sleep, but I'd felt stupid, and the few tears that escaped and burned down my cheeks did nothing to remove the barbed-wire-wrapped boulder that seemed to be sitting where I used to have a heart and a stomach. After curling up around the pain for a while, I'd rolled onto my back to look at the little sliver of sky I could see through my bedroom window. I couldn't stop thinking about how Harrison just . . . hung up. Not mean or dramatic or anything, just . . . gone.

"Are you okay? Mom kind of ran out on you," Fallon said.

I shrugged, uncomfortable with the half-truth I'd told my mother, and my relief when she'd had to go. "I'm good. I know Mom has to work; I didn't need to talk to her."

Fallon gestured at herself. "Why would you talk to Mom when you have me? I mean, I've got experience, beauty, and brains right here."

I rolled my eyes. "Oh, goody," I said, watching as my sister settled herself cross-legged on the floor. "Eighth-grade Oprah's in the house."

Fallon grinned. "I know, right? But I'm even better, because I'm not, like, old." She straightened. "Okay, so, what's up with JC and Harrison?"

I gnawed my lip. "Well, it's kind of a long story," I stalled. "It's not important. Just . . . she wasn't in a good mood. I shouldn't have tried to talk to her."

Fallon nodded. "Okay . . . so, basically, you and JC aren't tight anymore. Got it."

I winced, and Fallon tilted her head curiously. "What?" she asked. "That's what it sounds like. Why is that such a huge deal?"

"It's not, I guess," I admitted. "I just didn't think JC and I wouldn't ever be friends."

Fallon wrinkled her face sympathetically. "It happens, though. Remember I used to hang out with Erin Wallace in sixth? And we did everything together?"

I drew up the covers around my shoulders. "Sort of."

"And then, in seventh, we didn't. No real reason, we just . . . changed it up. Now she hangs out with Laura Scheingart. We're still friends, but . . . you know. I got into doing photography club, and Erin played soccer."

I hadn't joined a sport or a club, though. JC had gotten a new kidney—and 6A had gotten a new class ambassador. It wasn't at all the same.

"Do you think it's . . ." I hesitated. "Well, Leilani's Hawaiian, and JC's Filipino. Do you think JC likes Leilani more than me because I'm not Pacific Islander?"

Fallon widened her eyes. "Really, Serena? Really?"

I scowled. "Don't judge! I'm just saying!"

"How do you explain you two being best friends when you were in Ms. Daquila's class in fourth grade?" Fallon asked. "She's Filipino, and you and JC were always complaining about how strict she was, and how she always wrote your names on the board for talking. And wasn't Sylvia Finley's little sister, Sami, in your class too? Their family's from

Fiji, right? That's an island in the Pacific. Was she besties with JC too?"

"Okay, okay," I exclaimed. When I said the words out loud, they did sound stupid—and insecure, which was exactly how I felt. I sighed. "Do you think it's because I'm younger? Or because of this?" I gestured to my flat front. "I mean, JC already has fancy underwear, and she *has* to wear a bra. Not like me."

"Serena." Fallon groaned. "Be real. Nobody controls how fast their body grows. And if that *is* why JC is being weird, isn't she too dumb to want to be friends with?"

"Yeah, yeah, I know." I sighed, gloomy again. "I just wish I knew what I did."

Fallon made an exasperated noise. "Who says you did anything? Who says JC did? Dude, this is just"—she gestured helplessly—"school. I swear, there's nothing wrong with you, this is just how it goes for everyone. People change up and hang with someone else and that's what happens. Don't take it personally. Just . . . go out and be social, be fun. And boom, you'll find someone else to hang with. You won't even be thinking about JC—you'll be too busy having other friends. I promise, that's how it goes."

"I guess," I said, not able to imagine how it could be true. All the girls in 6A already had people to hang out with, and I didn't like the cliquey girls in 6B. I guessed I could make friends with one of the seventh graders, but what would we have in common, really?

Fallon and I sat in silence for a moment before my sister rolled to her feet. "Well, I'm going to bed. I just wanted to say whatever you do, don't sit around and feel sorry for yourself, Ree. If JC's not your friend anymore, whatever. Find someone else. Hang out with Harrison. You *can* have guy friends, you know," she added at my surprised look. "They don't have cooties."

"*Duh*," I muttered, but my face was hot. Imaginary germs or not, I knew that Harrison Ballard was the *last* person at Brigid Ogan who would be willing to be my friend after this week. Ugh, just *ugh*. Sometimes that was all there was to say.

~ 16 ~

Rockstar Regrets

"WHOSE IDEA WAS THE mascot?" I leaned toward Eliana from my perch on the bottom step of the bleachers.

Eliana cupped a hand around her ear, and I repeated myself over the thunder of stomping feet, clapping, and the loud bassline echoing through the gymnasium. When she finally heard me, a grin lit up Eliana's face. "Mrs. Henry's idea," she yelled back.

I should have known. Mrs. Henry was like the dorkiest kindergartner about stuff like all-school pep rallies. Even now, she was standing next to our guests from the city and the Home/School Alliance doing a peppy old-lady dance as the eighth-grade Spirit Squad, in teal, white, and gray uniforms, strutted their stuff.

The whole school stood or sat on bleachers around the edges of the gym while in the middle of the large room, a strip of kind of red—well, kind of burgundy, really—carpet led to a makeshift stage with a podium and microphone. In the middle of the floor, the Spirit Squad led a chant of *"You! Me! We! Drug-free!"* while doing a complicated dance routine that involved a lot of turns, kicks, and sharp arm choreography. As they finished their cheer—"Let's (clap) be smart! (clap, clap) Don't ever start!" (clap clap)—our mascot ran across and did a series of handsprings, while the cheer squad moved into their final stunt, this one a three-tiered pyramid with shoulder sits.

Brigid Ogan's mascot was the Brigid Banshee, so someone on cheer squad had to practice dancing and leaping in the weird gray ninja suit, white face paint, and a gray hooded cape. Banshees are supposed to wail when someone is going to die. Maybe a group wailing thing made sense at football games, but it seemed a little off when we did it for the Red Ribbon Rally, although they *could* have made up a cheer about not doing drugs or the banshee would wail for you . . . Anyway, we all cheered as the squad waved their metallic teal poms and bounced off to the sidelines.

Mrs. Henry, in a spiffy red pantsuit with wide lapels, moved her totally embarrassing dance to the microphone as the music wrapped up. "Another round of applause for the spirit and enthusiasm of the Spirit Squad and the Brigid Banshee! Thank you all! And now, it's time to hear from our judges. Mr. Walsh, come on down!"

The "unbiased" panel of judges included a mix of faculty and local volunteers, like Mr. Walsh, who was a big-fake-smile-and-handshake politician running for school board or something. Mr. Walsh moved through the door awards, smiling and shaking hands with each of the winners. Third place went to Mrs. Lansing's first-period eighth graders for their three little pigs inspired door (brick wrapping paper and "Don't Huff! Don't Puff! Stay Away from That Stuff!" on a sign with some really ugly pigs). Second prize went to us in Mr. Van's room 6A, which was pretty surprising, since we'd just wrapped the door in toilet paper to make a big mummy with a sign that said, "Don't get wrapped up in drugs." It was pretty generic, but Hyung made some good spooky yellow eyes peeping out between strips of toilet paper, and Madison had added phrases like "Pugs Not Drugs" and "Cupcakes Not Coke" to the tissue in graffiti writing, so we all clapped for ourselves and for them.

The grand prize went to 8C's homeroom class, of course. Everybody knew they'd win. 8C's door had little manga-looking heads of Luke and Leia and the Star Wars alien, Admiral Ackbar, pointing at a syringe and a bottle of pills orbiting a round black space station with the warning, "It's a trap!" in huge letters. It was both cute and kind of funny.

Each winning class got a ribbon for their door, a box of snacks for their homeroom, a picture in the yearbook, and bragging rights, until next year.

After Mr. Walsh finished shaking hands and grinning, Mrs. Henry leaned toward the mic again. "And now, the Red Ribbon subcommittee will come on down and present the next award!"

"Serena! That's you," Eliana said, poking my leg when I didn't move.

I looked around and found Harrison almost all the way to the mic. Hastily, I jumped up and practically ran across the gym floor until I was standing almost behind Harrison. Mr. Walsh gave me a wink as I went past.

"Well, come on, Serena, don't be shy," Mrs. Henry boomed, tugging me forward. I braced. This was going to be *bad*. On the other side of the podium from Harrison I stood and fiddled with the hem of my denim skirt, looking out over the sea of faces.

"First of all, I want to commend the Student Senate for an absolutely wonderful Red Ribbon Week this year. Harrison and Serena stepped up and made this an amazing week. Let's give them a round of applause!"

I could see Fallon and Sharyn slouched against the back wall of the gym with their friends. Fallon looked supremely bored, and when she caught me looking, she crossed her eyes. Hiding a smirk, I looked away.

As Mrs. Henry kept talking about how great we were, I wanted to sink through the floor. From the front row, Mr. Howard, who was the yearbook sponsor, held up a camera and smiled encouragingly. *Jeez.* I glanced at Harrison, who was staring at me with a slight frown on his face.

I gave him a *"What?"* look, but he shook his head slightly, turning back to Mrs. Henry.

"Secondly, it is my pleasure to today to announce our first-annual Brigid Ogan Buoyancy

Award. Harrison, Serena, tell us about this brand-new award, and how it came about."

Harrison looked over questioningly, while I shook my head slightly, eyes wide. I couldn't pretend I had something planned this time.

Clearing his throat, Harrison stepped up to the mic. "Thank you. The Student Senate would like to acknowledge Leilani Camacho for her idea for this award, and for helping us give it a name. All of us know students who have had hard times, and we want to acknowledge those who give to our community and make a difference anyway. Throughout the semester, the senate will keep a ballot box open in each homeroom, and individual students can nominate another member of the Brigid Ogan community who they feel is buoyant like a balloon—staying up, even when life is pulling them down. The award will be presented during our WinterFest celebration. I'm proud that this award is getting started during my time on Student Senate. Um." The crowd shifted as Harrison fumbled in his pocket and pulled out a slip of paper. I studied my shoes as he began to read.

"The Student Senate also would also like to acknowledge a late addition to our group this semester, who jumped in to help make this a great week.

So thank you," Harrison stepped to the side and pointed back at me, "Serena St. John."

Feeling my face get warm, I looked out into the audience and gave an embarrassed wave. I wondered if Sunita had told Harrison he had to say thank you on behalf of the senate. I'll bet he wouldn't have done it by himself.

Mrs. Henry was back at the microphone, beaming. "Yes, thank you, Serena, for your work with the Student Senate and for making this a great and memorable week for everyone. And now, let's have all of our senators stand. These are your representatives, students, and they're doing a great job!"

Ugh. So I stood up front for a little longer. I smiled and said thank you to Mrs. Henry when the rally was over. I smiled, with a little knot in my stomach, while I stood with Harrison and Sunita and Mrs. Henry, while Mr. Howard took pictures for yearbook. I smiled, because that's what everyone expected.

By the end of the day, that bright, happy smile was making my face ache, but you know what the worst part was? With all of the smiling we were doing, Harrison never once looked at me and smiled back.

❧ 17 ❧

Signal Interference

I WAS WAITING FOR Mom to come out of the dry cleaners after our grocery run when she opened my door and dumped a pink bakery box on my lap. "Hold that," she instructed, and slammed my door.

"We're having *cake*? Ooh!" I crowed, sliding my thumbs under the box tabs.

"No, Serena, don't *breathe* on it!" my mother scolded, pressing a hand to the box lid before I could rip it open. She added, "We're going to dinner at the Gerardos' tonight."

I frowned. "Why are we going over there?" JC and I hadn't talked to each other in days.

"We're going because we were invited," Mom said. She signaled the turn for our street.

I felt a twinge of apprehension. Had Mom gotten us invited over? She knew JC and I weren't friends right now. What if she was trying to *fix* things with cake?

"*Mom*. You didn't *say* anything to Mr. and Mrs. Gerardo, did you?"

"Anything like what?" Mom backed expertly into our parking stall. "Let's get the groceries unpacked. I want you to put on a clean shirt before we go. They're expecting us at five thirty."

"Wait, Mom. I don't—"

"Hurry up, Rena-B." Mom popped the trunk and got out of the car.

In the end, I didn't just change my shirt—I also changed shoes, and changed my hair twice, finally settling on twisting it around my head, using my little fake pearl hairpins to anchor it where it stuck out. I dragged my feet getting to the car, but I hated being late anywhere. If the Gerardos were expecting us, walking in when they were hungry and mad about the delay wouldn't make anything better.

I was still nervous, though. "So, no special reason for dinner tonight?" I asked as we drove out of the neighborhood.

"Not that I know of, no," Mom said, and smiled.

"Your hair looks nice, Rena."

In spite of her smile, my misgivings grew wings and swooped through my stomach.

When Mrs. Gerardo opened the door, she was her usual self, her oval face smiling and welcoming, her bobbed dark hair tucked behind ears sporting yellow and red dangly earrings. "You're just in time," she said, taking the cake from Mom as she toed out of her loafers. "Are you hungry? Serena, go up to JC's room and tell the girls it's time to eat."

The *girls*? Oh no. I could *not* handle Leilani and her too-perfect self, not today.

Kicking off my shoes to join the pile in the entryway, I dragged myself up the stairs. I climbed loudly, thumping my feet on every riser. As soon as I reached the top, I began knocking on the wall and calling JC's name. I didn't want to get too close to her room and overhear her saying something terrible about me to Leilani.

"JC! Dinner!"

"Serena?" JC stood in her doorway, looking startled. "Hey."

"Hey. Your mom says it's time to eat." I shoved my hands in my pockets.

JC nodded, smoothing her hair behind her ears

as if she was a little nervous too. "Cool." She ducked into her room for a moment, her voice floating toward me through the open door. "You remember my *ate* Julia, right?" JC said, using the respectful Tagalog word for an older girl cousin.

A taller girl with her hair in a shiny knot atop her head stepped into the hallway looking at her phone. She shoved it into her pocket and smiled. "Hey, Serena," she said, and went down the stairs ahead of us.

"Oh! Julia! Wow, I didn't know you were here," I added, relief making me a little loud.

"She's here to look at schools," JC explained, starting down the stairs behind me. "She's trying to go to some arts high school in Oakland. Her parents think she should move in with us next semester."

"Oh, really? Wow." I glanced over my shoulder to see JC's expression. Julia was an eighth grader. It was weird to think of her leaving home already to go to school.

JC's dad and Julia's mom were siblings, and Julia and JC were the two youngest girl cousins in their large, mostly boy-cousins family. The story was that toddler Julia had stolen baby JC's bottle once, and Mr. Gerardo joked that they'd each been competing to have the biggest bottle ever since. And it *was* a competition. Julia surfed at home on Oahu, but JC was on a swim team at home in California. Julia got the best grades in math, but JC got better grades in language arts. Julia was two inches taller, but JC's hair was four inches longer. Mrs. Gerardo was always telling JC she should be more like her ate Julia, which meant that JC kind of hated her cousin, even though Julia was always pretty nice. And now they'd be living in the same house for a school year? *Whoa.*

"Tatay said it'll be just like having a sister." JC's voice was way too cheery.

I winced. My sister was a pain a lot of the time, but at least I knew she loved me, even when she ditched me to go to Sharyn's house. I tried to think of something comforting to say. "Well, just remember, if it's not fun, it's a *growing* experience," I whispered, reminding JC of one of Mr. Van's favorite sayings.

"Yay, growing." JC wiggled her fingers in sarcastic joy.

I laughed, feeling a little less weird about being at JC's house. Between surgery, a new best friend, and Julia moving in, things had to feel a little bit strange for JC. Maybe being with an old friend for dinner wouldn't feel like a bad visit from the past, but a good one.

The meal was loud and busy, with plates and platters passing round. Mrs. Gerardo complimented Julia on the Caesar salad dressing and told her she should give JC the recipe. Mom told Mrs. Gerardo how much she liked the woven placemats Mrs. Gerardo had gotten from the Philippines, and Mrs. Gerardo told her she'd tell her where to find some. Mr. Gerardo kept trying to get me to eat a little more of the delicious fried rice. Mom asked Mrs. Gerardo how plans were coming for JC's birthday, which started a playful argument between JC and her dad about what JC wanted and how much he was going to spend. Mom asked Julia how she was finding Oakland schools, and that reminded Mrs. Gerardo of something.

"You girls have a project soon—those WinterFest birdies, right?" Mrs. Gerardo asked suddenly. "When do you start work on that? It's almost November! Only five weeks left!"

My stomach clenched. I shot JC a quick look across the table. "Um . . ."

"No, don't ask them when they're working, tell them to get to work," Mr. Gerardo interrupted, waving his hand. "Always, Jojo comes crying at the last minute. No—this time, we'll choose our design

and get started tonight," he decided. "No last minute this time."

"I used to do that, JC," Julia said, and laughed
self-consciously. "I cut it too-too close one time and
lost fifty points on my project! I turn in everything
early now."

I gave JC another wary look, but she was busy
scowling at her father. "I do not always come crying
to you," she interrupted, ignoring her cousin. "Jeez,
you make me sound like I'm some kind of baby,
Tatay."

Mr. Gerardo laughed. "Yes, you do cry, and you're
my baby, so that's all right, huh?"

Now both parents were chuckling indulgently at
JC's furious protests while Julia looked at her plate
and rolled her eyes.

But all of this was missing the point. Was JC going
to just ignore what her mother had said and pretend
everything was the same as always?

"Weren't you girls doing projects on your own
this year?" Mom was studying my face. "Or did you
change your mind, Rena-Bean? I thought JC had
decided to make owl magnets with . . . Leilani?"

I glowered, trying to shush Mom. I wasn't ready
to hear JC talk about Leilani. Why did Mom have

to mention her in front of everyone? I shot a look at JC, but she was still sulking, arms crossed, glaring at her plate.

"What's this, anak?" Mrs. Gerardo's perfectly plucked eyebrows raised as she questioned her daughter. "Magnets?"

When I looked back at Mom, her steady gaze held knowledge and understanding I hadn't expected. "What's it going to be, Rena?" she asked softly.

It sounded like Mom was asking me about more than my WinterFest project.

I chewed on my bottom lip, remembering what Mrs. Henry had said about taking the opportunity to stand up and speak out. Wasn't doing the vlogs reminding me to tell my own stories? Why was I waiting for JC to tell me mine?

I took a deep breath. "You're right, Mom," I said, my voice only a little shaky. "JC decided to do magnets with Leilani."

Mrs. Gerardo turned to JC, her expression disbelieving. "When your father already brought home all the concrete and supplies you asked for, for the bird's bath?"

"I changed my mind, Nanay," JC muttered, still sulking.

I looked down the table at JC, looking at her hand where it gripped her fork, while her other hand was twisting a strand of her hair like mad. Her nails were still bitten down and still painted with glitter polish. JC looked tired and upset, which made me wonder, what if the birdbath had seemed like it was too big a project? Maybe JC was looking for a smaller project because she still felt so sick that a big project like a birdbath felt like she'd never get it done.

"It's okay, JC. It's fine," I said, and JC looked up at me with a small, watery smile.

"Such a waste of money," Mrs. Gerardo was complaining, shaking her head.

"I have receipts; we can take the supplies back," Mr. Gerardo soothed her. "Artists always change their minds," he added with a grin. "What about you, Serena? You change your mind too?"

"You'll have to wait and see," I said, trying to look mysterious.

JC blinked. "Wait, so you're not doing bird magnets?" she asked. "Didn't you say you were going to look for some different birds on Artistly, like flamingos?"

That's what she'd *told me* to do. No one said I had to *do* it.

I shook my head, more certain now. "Nope."

I still didn't know *what* I was going to do, but for the first time I was a tiny bit relieved not to be doing it with JC's input. I'd loved the big, fancy birdbath we'd planned on, and it had hurt—a lot—when she didn't want to do it anymore. But now I was free to do anything I wanted, without anyone's input. To be me, without looking at what anyone else was doing.

What was the worst that could happen? It might be terrible. It might be a disaster.

But it might not.

SERENA|SAYS

Good Eeeeeevening, Vorrrld! It's Halloweeeeeen!

[scary, maniacal laughter]

Okay, that was bad.

What's up, World? It IS Halloween, and this is *Serena Says* . . . Storytime!

Welcome back to my vlog! Today's Halloween—and it's been weird. First, I couldn't figure out what to wear. I was just going to skip it, but yesterday someone asked Mr. Van what he was wearing, and he said he was getting out his "This Is My Costume" shirt, and, okay, NO. I knew I couldn't be that lame. So last night, I was digging through the hall closet when I saw Mom's old red Christmas hat with the white pom-pom on it. I asked her if I could take off the pom-pom, and then I wore it, plus my big red fleece hoodie and Fallon's red sweats. I even wore red sneakers. And I was Peter from *The Snowy Day*! I loved that book when I was little!

Which is a good thing, since I had to carry it around all day because almost no one knew who I was supposed to be.

I HATE IT when that happens.

You know who the only person was who got my costume—I mean, besides Ms. Pettinelli, our school librarian? Leilani. I KNOW, right? She said it was her favorite book when she was little, too, because she'd never seen snow, and she wanted to really, really badly. She begged her parents for a red snowsuit, even though they lived in Pensacola. Cute, huh?

I KNOW.

It's weird for me to think of her as . . . a little kid, someone adorable and funny, and not someone super perfect and annoying. Honestly, I know what I said about first impressions, but I kind of hate having to change how I think about anyone.

Take Mrs. Vejar. At the beginning of the year, everyone thought she was SO MEAN. She gives a test Every. Single. Wednesday. And she actually has a copy of the dress code on her bulletin board, and she CHECKS IT. I mean, seriously? But then she started to do something called Top-Up Thursdays, where we do kind of a class project and get participation points to help raise our scores if we forgot to study or don't do so well on the Wednesday test. It's actually saved my bacon a couple of times now. So even though I didn't want to, I kind of really like her now. She's nicer than she seemed at first.

For today's Top-Up Thursday, Mrs. Vejar moved two desks up to the front of the room, facing the class. Then she wrote, "Behind the mask, you are . . ." and then had two people come up and sit with their backs to the whiteboards. Everyone else had to go up and write a complimentary statement about them on the board behind them. After everyone got through, each person stood up, and she took their picture in front of all of their words. She said it would help us each remember that we are more than who we think we are.

Sometimes it was funny, but a lot of people were kind of almost crying and stuff. And then, near the end of class, Mrs. Vejar pointed to Luis Archega, and all of his friends kind of laughed and made stupid noises. Luis made a big deal of getting up, and then he kind of, like, stared at everyone, like he was daring them to say something he didn't like.

I didn't know what to say. Luis is really cute and popular, but he's kind of mean—probably because his brother, Roberto, is maybe a little mean to him. I knew that, but all I could think about was him doing those barking sounds when I was sick, and everyone laughing at me . . .

His friends—and all the girls who think he's hot—went up and wrote stuff like "You're so cool" and "Nice" and stuff, but I was stuck. And then Leilani got up. And she wrote, "Behind the mask, you are the guy who keeps everyone laughing so hard they don't remember what was bugging them."

It's true, but it just . . . it took something I didn't like about Luis and made it . . . kind.

I finally got up right before the bell and wrote that I liked the way he mostly smiles with one side of his face, because he's got a super-unique grin. Which is maybe kind of random, but whatever—it's true. And when he stood up and read everything on the board, while Mrs. Vejar took his picture, he just looked . . . kind of surprised. Then kind of like he was thinking, you know?

Probably not because I said he had a nice smile, but . . . I can't stop thinking about what Leilani did. She really figured out how to find . . . a good thing in a kind of annoying thing. Which kind of makes me feel like I should think about her maybe a little more . . . Maybe she's kind of an awesome person in an annoying package too?

So, ANYWAY! Does your school do Top-Up Thursdays or something like it? Do you have a kid like Luis in your class? If you were sitting in front of the whiteboard, what would you want someone to write about you? Serena says you can dress up for Halloween but still be yourself.

That's my story, and I'm out.

Also, note to self: no weird laughs or voices in the vlogs.

❧ 18 ❧

A Crack in the Wall

SINCE NOBODY KNEW WHO I was anyway, after school I changed costumes and put on the one that I wore just about every year. The problem with wearing Mom's scrubs on a night in October was that, even when it had been nice out during the day, after sundown, in a car with the engine off, the thin, cotton material did *nothing* to fight the cold. Mom had been inside for a half hour already, and even huddled in her lab coat, my hands were getting too cold to text. I was getting shivers.

The parking lot of New Vista Behavioral Health Center was mostly deserted, since it was after business hours, but there was a sprinkling of cars in the field of painted lines. Mom had parked right up front in some doctor's space, so I was under one of the fancy streetlights, which flickered creepily as the wind-tossed branches created shadows.

We were *supposed* to be at the mall by now. Trick-or-Treat Street only went on from five to seven thirty, before NewPark became a regular mall again, just one with a bunch of extra security guards wandering around to shoo out the teens who were hanging around while they took down the haunted house. If Mom didn't hurry up, I wouldn't get to trick-or-treat at all—it was already six thirty.

My phone chimed with a text from MAMA MIA.

Going to be another ten minutes or so. Sorry.

"Oh, come on!" I moaned, my head falling back against the headrest with an annoyed thump. I wanted candy, but at this rate, I was going to get to hit only *one* store. I sighed and unlocked my seat belt, zipping up my jacket before stomping out of the car. There was no way I was going to sit out here another minute and freeze in my stupid costume. I typed back with chilly thumbs.

Waiting in lobby so I don't freeze/die.

I got back Mom's smiley face as I chose the set of heavy glass doors off to the left and tugged my way into the building. New Vista's administrative offices were warm and quiet, and nowhere near the staff-only areas where patients stayed, and where Mom probably was.

I breathed out a sigh as heat bathed my cheeks. The banks of fluorescent bulbs above the receptionist's computers were dim, but light shone behind the closed window of the financial office, illuminating a path through clusters of low tables, benches, and chairs in the L-shaped waiting room. I headed for the elbow of the L, as far away from the cold night air as I could get, and pulled up a cushy seat right beneath the heating register. *Bliss.* Now it didn't matter how long Mom took. Mostly. She told us every year we could just get cheap candy the day *after* Halloween, but THAT was NOT the point.

I had my feet propped against the wall, trying to successfully match different-colored jewels on my tiny phone screen when the lobby doors opened again. The sound of someone plopping down in one of the leather chairs by the reception desk, and a snap as a tiny lamp came on piqued my curiosity. What sounded like a suitcase opening interested me even more.

I slipped my phone into my back pocket, bored and nosy enough to fake a need for the water fountain.

Once there, I held my toy stethoscope down and slurped noisily, then took the few extra steps necessary to peep around the corner.

What I saw had me pulling back and silently smacking my own forehead.

Plugged in to the base of the lobby lamp sat a laptop, on top of a familiar brown briefcase to make it a little higher. He was logging in to the hospital's guest Wi-Fi page, and he had a box of Red Vines on the table in front of him.

It was stupid to hide. Blowing out a breath, I stepped out from behind the corner.

"Harrison?"

Harrison didn't even jump. He just sighed and glanced over his shoulder. "Serena."

Nope, this was *not* super awkward *at all*.

"Um, what are you doing here?" I blurted, then bit down on my tongue until my eyes watered. Could I sound any more brainless? "I mean, I see your laptop; are you going to watch a movie?"

"No," Harrison said, then shrugged and added, "Mom and Dad are with Lance. My brother?" His brows raised, as if I needed reminding.

"Yeah, I remember your brother's here. I'm waiting for my mom," I offered.

"Yep." Harrison fiddled with his laptop again.

"So I guess you're not going out tonight," I said, stating the obvious.

"Nope."

From his one-word answers, I knew Harrison didn't want to talk; slime molds could probably tell that, and Mrs. Vejar told us they don't actually have brains. But part of me felt like being annoying. He shouldn't still be acting weird with me. I'd apologized, hadn't I?

I crossed the room and dropped into the upholstered chair next to Harrison.

"Did you finish making your virus flash cards yet?" I asked. "I can quiz you."

"I'm not doing flash cards," Harrison said, scrolling through a website.

I leaned forward to see what he was reading. It was so boring that I couldn't help myself. "Jeez, Harrison, are you reading the *newspaper*? See, this is why no one ever calls you Harry."

Now that I'd said them out loud, the words didn't sound as good as they had in my head. Mr. Howard would have called them a non sequitur. That sounded fancy, but it just meant it made zero sense.

It didn't impress Harrison, either, who glared.

"Serena, what do you want?"

I opened my mouth, then closed it again. I didn't know why I was bugging him. What did I actually want?

I didn't really know Harrison, but he was part of . . . life, at school. Like the walls and the bulletin boards and the desks. Without Harrison insulting me, I felt . . . a space, like a chair out of place, one I kept tripping over, and stubbing my toe. Why wouldn't he forgive me? He was only mad because he said *I* was treating *him* like *he* had a disease. How could anyone catch mental health issues from just talking about his brother? Was that a thing?

All I wanted was for *him* to stop treating *me* like I was the disease. For everything to go back to the way it was.

"I want to know about your brother," I blurted. "And you. And your family, and stuff."

"JC wants to know, or you?" Harrison asked, his mouth tightening.

I swallowed. I kind of deserved that. "You don't have to say anything. You just . . . can. If you want to."

Harrison shrugged, his eyes on his computer screen.

I chewed the inside of my cheek. Should I apologize again? Should I leave Harrison alone? I tried to think of what Fallon would say if she was here. I couldn't think of anything.

My phone vibrating in my back pocket had me jumping up in relief. I flipped open my phone to see a new message.

On my way.

Excellent. If we hurried, I'd still have twenty minutes to collect my haul.

I took two steps toward the door and stopped.

"Um, Harrison?" My mouth was weirdly dry.

Harrison nodded to my phone. "Yeah, I know. That's your mom. Bye."

"Um, wait. We're going to Trick-or-Treat Street. Do you want to ask your mom and dad if you can go? My mom can drop you off back here, no problem."

Harrison's eyebrows rumpled as he frowned. He looked confused, then suspicious. "No. Thank you."

My throat pinched. He was still treating me like a disease, but at least I'd tried. "Okay. See you tomorrow."

"Hey, Hobbit?" Harrison said as I pushed on the heavy glass.

The old nickname expanded my lungs with a rush of hope. I half-turned toward Harrison, tense with cautious optimism. "What?"

"Nobody will believe a Hobbit is a doctor, you know. You're just too short."

"Shut *up*, you giant boy mutant," I scoffed, but I couldn't keep from grinning.

～ 19 ～

Minding Our Beeswax

WORKING IN GROUPS AT school is *the WORST*. Someone always messes around, and someone *else* always only wants everyone to use their ideas. A couple of busy bees always end up doing most of the work, and even then, we still don't always get an A. In social studies, Mr. Baumgartner, who loves groups, always chooses them himself, which today means I have Eliana in my group—yay!—and Mateo and Ally, who are fine; Cameron, who is kind of a slacker; and . . . Leilani.

Oof.

Even the handful of Fresca candies Eliana stuck in my pocket when my desk was next to hers didn't make things better, though that candy is my favorite.

Leilani Camacho—everywhere I look, every time I turn around. There. She. Is.

After we all moved our desks, Mr. B handed each group a pack of worksheets. "Fifteen minutes to come up with a project and rough out your first five steps to making it happen, people," he called.

A buzz rose as students read the project instructions. Across from me, Cameron thumped his head on his desk, brown hair flopping across his eyes. "Aw, *man!*"

I kept my complaint silent, but as I paged through the assignment, I agreed. We'd been studying ancient civilizations since school started, and the clay tablets and cuneiform were okay, but we'd recently moved from Mesopotamia to ancient Egypt's Nile Crescent—and Mr. B was *obsessed.* He was way too hyped about floods, pharaohs, and mummies. Aside from our other worksheets and vocabulary pages, the Egypt project was worth 25 percent of our semester grade. Our projects were also going to be on display in the school library the night of WinterFest—now only FOUR. *WEEKS. AWAY.* I rubbed my arms, pretty sure the buzz I felt was panic, and not excitement.

"This doesn't look that bad," Ally said after

a moment. "We just have to pick one project out of six. Listen, there's 'create a game show; write and perform a play or skit; create a topical map of ancient Egypt, compare to a topical map of Egypt today; write and illustrate a children's book; make an illustrated timeline on a three-panel display board'—Ew, no," Ally interjected, then continued, "'create a TV spot or news report, interviewing a relevant person; compose a song and create a music video; make a shoebox museum with at least two dioramas.' We have two due dates before the final one. That's not bad at all."

"Oh, sure, it's just one project, but we also have to make notes on how we do our research, *and* how much time we're in the library, *and* write up what we used for our projects, and why we chose them—plus do all our *other* homework. This blows," Mateo griped.

"At least we get to work on it during class. I have piano recital this weekend, so if anyone wants to get together, it's going to have to wait," Eliana volunteered.

"Do you see the grading stuff? We're not just graded by Mr. B. We're also getting a pass/fail from Ms. Pettinelli for research skills in the library, and letter grades from Mr. Howard for language arts or from Mrs. Vejar for science!" I scowled.

"Ooh! Where do you see that?" Eliana sounded happier than she should have. "Hey! We get to present our projects to third graders! So cool! That's way better than just parents."

Better? I was ready to argue Eliana's point of view when Leilani confidently tossed the silky tassel of her ponytail over her shoulder. "Guys. I know how we can do the game show."

"Who says we're doing a game show?" I argued, then bit my lip. While *I* wanted to film the news report and the interview, maybe not everyone did. What if everyone else wanted a game show? "I mean, whatever, if you want to do one, but I don't watch game shows," I added.

"Game shows are kind of meh," Ally agreed, and I breathed a sigh of relief. "I think we should vote on what we do."

"Yeah," Cameron chimed in. "I wanted to make a mummy. Wouldn't that be cool, if we did a map, and had the mummy running across the—"

"No. No mummies." Eliana shook her head, speaking loudly over Cameron's complaints. "Mummies are basic. We need something more interesting."

"Like what?" Lani challenged. "My brothers can help me program us a cool game in Scratch on my laptop, and—"

"But your brothers aren't in our group," Mateo pointed out. "Read, right there on the first page. Mr. B says, 'no outside help from family or friends.' And, anyway, what are the rest of us supposed to do while your brothers are making the game?"

"Exactly. So let's vote. That way, each of us gets a job, and gets to do it without anyone interrupting or showing up and taking over," I said too loudly. As our ex–class ambassador, job-stealing was still kind of a sore point for me.

"Nobody's going to take over," Eliana the Peacemaker said, giving me a warning look. "We should probably find something we can all work on together. Right, Lani?"

"Fine, but it would have been cool." Lani sounded sulky.

"We could do a play," Ally suggested. "We could wear eyeliner and black wigs and—"

"Hold up. What are Mateo and I supposed to wear in this play?" Cameron demanded.

"I'm not wearing a stupid diaper, a skirt, or a dress," Mateo announced.

"Um . . . well . . . ," Ally said, flipping through her social studies book.

Lani scowled. "It's a loincloth, not a diaper. And that's not what Egyptians wore. Look at the pharaohs. They—"

"Still not doing it," Mateo said, arms crossed. "Let's just write a book and call it a day."

"A *children's* book," Eliana corrected him. "If you write a book, it has to be good for, like, eight year olds."

"That's easy," Ally said. "We just tell them what's in our social studies book."

"And they'll be so bored they'll die yawning," Cameron griped. "Can't I please draw one mummy?"

I rolled my eyes. "Yes, Cameron, fine! Draw all the mummies! Do an entire chapter on mummies and those gross whatever jars . . . and you can draw it unraveling, so you can write about how and why they mummified people."

"Cool," Cameron said, looking pleased. "Canopic jars!"

"Yeah, that's cool. But what am I doing?" Mateo demanded.

"Uh—" I glanced at Ally and Eliana. Weren't they going to say something? But no, they seemed to be waiting for . . . me. I swallowed. "Uh, you're always rapping, Mateo, so maybe you can take everyone's facts, and kind of, um, give them flow? Make them rhyme?" At his widening eyes, I added, "Not, like, all the way, you don't have to make a perfect rap for all of them, that's a lot of work, but just . . . make them sound less lame?"

I turned back to the group. "And, um, maybe we should all have, like, three facts, so our book is, like, eighteen pages long, plus the front and back cover, so it's twenty pages? So then it's even numbers, and it'll work better."

"That makes sense," Ally said, writing quickly. "So each of us researches and writes up our facts, like one fact per page? And Cameron is illustrating them?"

"Hey, not all of them," Cameron protested. "You can draw too, Ally."

"You're a good artist," I agreed, and Ally ducked her head, beaming. "Eliana, you could be in charge of the actual bookmaking—you know, choose paper and connect the pages and all of that stuff." I smiled at Eliana. She smiled back but cupped her left hand around her right hand. With her right hand, she pointed at Lani.

Oh yeah. *Her.*

"And, um, Lani," I swallowed as Lani raised a brow expectantly. What did she like to do? What was she good at? I didn't know. Lani wasn't my business.

"Lani, you're the printer, I think?" My voice cracked. "You can type up the project description, and run spell-check, and maybe help fact-check everybody's pages so they're perfect? And you know how Ms. Pettinelli likes everybody to cite sources . . . I'll help with that, and I'll work on the cover design, and we'll put it all together."

"Cool. We'll do it together," Eliana said. "The cover and the typing and the book, right? My dad has a laminator. We can get wallpaper samples and make an actual cover."

I shrugged. "Sounds good. I mean, if Lani wants to . . ."

"Well, okay," Lani said reluctantly. "I'm a pretty good typist, and I could figure out a laminator . . . I think. Fine with me, I guess."

I exhaled. "Okay, good. Is that everybody?"

"So you're group leader," Ally asked, writing something down on her paper.

"Um . . . ?" I looked as Ally pointed at the board.

Across the whiteboard, Mr. B had scrawled: *Group leader's name. Project Name. Individual steps 1–5 for your group project.*

I looked around the circle at my classmates. I wasn't a leader. That was something Lani would be good at, or what JC or people like Erik or Sunita did. I was just . . . a regular worker bee in the group, just getting organized . . . right? What would a group leader do? Or was I the one who decided that? If I didn't decide, was I not taking an opportunity to raise my voice, like Mrs. Henry said? "Um," I cleared my throat and made a lightning-quick decision. "I'll be group leader, if everyone wants."

"Good, 'cause I already wrote you down. In pen," Mateo added, leaning over his paper.

Around me, everyone was writing.

"Seven minutes," Mr. B called.

"The first step is to choose our facts," I said thoughtfully.

"I need to research," Eliana muttered around the end of her pencil.

"Step two," I suggested.

Ally looked up. "Good idea," she said. "The library next."

Around the circle, heads nodded, eyes focused. I

took a deep breath. I had no idea what to do next. I'd never been a group leader, not when JC had been around to be funnier and louder and more confident than everyone. Could I really do this?

What if I could?

～20～

The Way the Cookies Crumble

THE NEXT FRIDAY, MOM got off early to take Fallon and me to the dentist. While waiting for the hygienist to finish polishing my molars with bubblegum-flavored tooth polish—*so* nasty—Mom and Fallon wandered through the little Arden Station Mall next door, which had a kitchen store, art gallery, and antique shop.

From the antique shop, Mom bought a massive rhinestone ring, which I knew was for my grandmother, Bibi—who had one of those weird pairs of ceramic hands on her dresser with all the fingers wearing bling. (Our grandfather, Poppy, said Bibi was really a magpie in human form.) Instead of shopping for holiday presents like Mom, Fallon bought herself a pair of costume glasses with plain glass lenses. They were, Fallon said, Superman glasses, though the heavy black plastic frames didn't seem to give Fallon the urge to fly off to Krypton.

Unfortunately.

"I love these. I look even smarter than I am," Fallon said, preening in the car's mirror. She angled her camera for a selfie.

I leaned into the shot and bared my teeth, rubbing my tongue over their weirdly slick, freshly cleaned surfaces. "They're too big. Your red cat-eyed glasses were better."

"They were cute before the arm broke, weren't they?" Fallon said thoughtfully. "I'll have to do something with them for my WinterFest basket. Maybe I'll glue them to something. Do you think they'd make a cute magnet? Or maybe a pin?"

I slumped, suddenly not as excited by my teeth anymore. *Magnets. WinterFest.* UGH. Three weeks, twenty-one days away, and *STILL* no project. This was the WORST year ever.

The whole of eighth grade had chosen a single theme—Red Hot Winter—for their charity baskets. Everything they added could be anything red, anything hot—or anything wintry. This gave them

TONS of stuff to choose. Red Hots. Furry white mittens and red-and-white fleece quilts. Sriracha sauce. Spicy nuts. Every time I thought about it, I got annoyed all over again. Fallon's basket was going to be super *easy!* Whose feather-headed idea was it for 6A to do birds?

"You'd better call Mr. Gerardo and tell him you need to start on the birdbath," Fallon said, as if she were reading my mind.

"I told you, I'm not doing a birdbath," I reminded her. "I haven't picked a project yet."

"You'd better pick something," my sister warned. "We have to write down what we're donating before Thanksgiving break."

"Jeez, I *know*," I said, waving my hand to shush her. "I've got three weeks left, all right?" I was getting tired of how everyone wanted to solve my project problem for me. Even Mom was giving me hints every day now, leaving pages torn out of magazines on my bed, or showing me articles on her phone. If people would just leave me alone, I'd come up with something. Eventually.

"How's that social studies project coming?" Mom asked, and I sighed loudly, wishing I could shush her too.

"Excuse me, but how come you never ask Fallon about *her* projects?"

"'Cause I'm so fabulous, no one needs to worry about me." Fallon patted her own back, and I wondered if people really could break their arms doing that, like Poppy always said.

"Social studies class isn't the problem," I said. "It's Cameron. If he doesn't stop playing on the internet in the library when we're supposed to be looking up our Egypt facts, he's going to make our whole group lose points."

"I remember my sixth-grade group project," said Fallon gloomily. "We got a B-minus because Mindy Norton forgot to bring the cover she was working on, so we didn't turn it in on time."

"La-la-la, don't tell me," I sang, putting my hands over my ears as we turned into the parking lot of Lunardi's Market. "I don't want to hear all the ways this could get even worse. I'm the group leader, and this is going to WORK."

"That's the right attitude," Mom said, smiling. "Okay, girls. Do we need any lunch things? Bread? More almond butter? I'm just going in to pick up some oatmeal and salad stuff."

"Dill pickles for me," Fallon said, adding, "please."

"I'll go in with you," I volunteered, and hopped out of the car. "We need cookies."

My mother rolled her eyes. "Nice try, Rena. Didn't you hear what the hygienist said?"

"Whatever, I'll floss more. I just want one bag of gingersnaps," I pleaded, following her across the parking lot. "Or we could get those lemon ices you like? Or—" I stopped, briefly distracted from begging by a huge display of pie pumpkins, squashes, gourds, and colorful dried corn outside the grocery store.

"I don't know why anyone likes those," I said, regarding the lumpy vegetables. "They look diseased."

"Mmm," Mom said, eyeing a pair of potted mums decorated with burlap ribbon.

"I mean, people buy them every year. They get all gross . . . but if you buy us cookies, we'll use those right away," I added, picking up a crook-necked gourd and turning it sideways. "This looks like a bird."

Mom decided on the mums and picked them up. She flicked me a glance. "Mmm," she said again. "Did you want to make a turkey or something for your raffle basket with that?"

"Uh, no," I said, putting it down. "How would I do that?"

"I don't know," Mom said, going into the store. "You girls are the artsy ones. I just buy the glue."

After she picked up what she'd come for, Mom surprised me by stopping in the baking aisle and searching through the packaged baking tools until she found what she was looking for. "There," she said, pointing at a metal cookie cutter. "You could make some decorated bird sugar cookies and be done with the whole thing."

"*Mother,*" I began, teeth gritted—then stopped. No, I didn't know what I wanted to do for my project, and there were only three weeks left. Yes, I should pick something soon. Yes, even bird cookies would do. But my stubbornness clung like ropes of cement, hardening around my feet. I tried to get unstuck from the feelings by reminding myself that Mom was just trying to help, but it wasn't working.

"Rena-B?" Mom said patiently. "Let's get it over with, okay?"

"*Fine.*" The *f* hissed out like a leaking tire. "I'll make sugar cookies."

"There," Mom said, picking up two of the vaguely bird-shaped cutters. "That wasn't so hard, was it?

And we've got all kinds of food coloring and flour and sugar at home. Now just pick a day to do it, and you're good. One less thing to worry about."

I jerked my shoulders in a shrug. Great. Except it wasn't *Mom's* project to worry about.

I slumped down in the back seat on the way home, looking out the window at the lines of cars driving past. For the first time this school year, Fallon and I didn't have to stay with our neighbor, Mrs. Kaur, or do Homework Club. With Fallon in eighth grade, Mom had decided to let us be home alone, as long as we were responsible, didn't invite anyone over, and got our homework done. Homework Club at school cost money, and if Mom didn't have to pay for it, she didn't want to.

I knew it was really, *really* important to Mom that we did our homework and didn't mess up, just because an adult wasn't there to watch us. I knew I had to do my project, and turn it in on time, or we might have to go back to afterschool care. Mom would be disappointed, and Fallon would basically kill me. But it was still really, really important to do my project *my* way.

Which meant that there was NO way I was making any stupid sugar cookies.

SERENA|SAYS

What's up, World? It's your girl Serena. Welcome back to my vlog!

Serena Says is BOOKISH! Books are the one thing in the world to pick up when your brain needs a break from . . . basically everything. Bibi signed me up for a book subscription box last Christmas, which was probably the best gift I got. This month, I got *New Kid* by Jerry Craft, and I LOVE, love, love it.

Okay, so first of all, *New Kid* by Jerry Craft is a graphic novel about Jordan Banks, a seventh grader who is a really good cartoonist, and his parents think that's nice and all, but what they're really excited about is how smart he is so they send him to a really fancy private school.

Jordan wants to go to art school. That's all he's EVER wanted. Unfortunately, Riverdale Academy Day School is NOT an art school, and it is full of people who are kind of rude, in racial ways, if you know what I mean. Teachers call him the wrong names, because they get him mixed up with other black boys. And when people talk about minorities, or slavery, or anything about the civil rights movement or black history or black people at all? Everyone stares at him. Also, everyone thinks he can play sports because that's a stereotype about black people.

So, anyway, there are some good things at Jordan's school, like the food and some of the teachers, and Jordan eventually makes two really good friends, but he still has weird days sometimes, and weird conversations with other kids, and teachers that make him feel . . . basically weird . . . and uncomfortable, and sometimes mad. His friends from his old school aren't sure he likes them anymore, and sometimes he isn't sure how to be friends with both his old friends and his new ones. It turns out that being the new kid isn't the problem—being quiet about it is the problem. Jordan has to start, like, taking chances and saying what's wrong and what's bothering him, before things get better.

So what about you? Have you ever felt weird at school because of something someone assumed about you? Have you ever assumed something about someone . . . and then maybe told people? What do you do if you can't solve a problem with your friends? Remember, even if it's not in a book, your story is important too. Serena says your whole life can change if you take chances and speak up about the things that matter to you.

That's MY story, and I'm out . . .

This vlog was AMAZING. I really need to start uploading these pretty soon.

21

Diva Drama

"MOM! MOM!" I RACED into the kitchen, my heart pounding so hard I felt sick. "JC's back in the hospital!"

We'd spent Mom's weekend off prepping the house for the season, including raking the leaves from our postage-stamp backyard, batting down cobwebs, and washing all the windows. Mom always says, "Family time is offline," so even though I'd finally gotten to upload a vlog to Fallon's channel, I hadn't gotten time to look at texts or check email until way late Sunday night, and then I'd been too sleepy to look—and now, Monday morning. Disaster.

"Is she?" Mom looked startled, putting down the

banana she was breaking into her smoothie. "When did that happen?"

"Eliana forwarded a text Sunita got from Lani last night," I panted, showing Mom the phone. "It says right here, 'Just heard JC's in the hospital with a viral infection.'"

"Oh, that's too bad," Mom said sympathetically. "When immune-suppressing drugs do their job, the body doesn't reject the transplant, but it's left susceptible to every virus and—"

I was worried and upset, and Mom wanted to teach me how immune drugs worked *now*? "I know all that," I blurted. "But if JC's in the hospital, why didn't anyone call me?"

"Oh," Mom said, sounding less sure of herself. "Well, that I don't know."

I didn't know either, and the more I thought about it, the harder I freaked. The messages scrolled by: JC had been fine on Friday. Lani had been over Friday night. JC felt retchy on Saturday. JC had had a fever Saturday night. JC had told Lani she wasn't going to the ER, so she hadn't told her parents. JC had woken up her parents at 3:00 a.m., and they'd had to take her *immediately*; because she was so weak, she had fainted and fallen on the floor.

Almost everyone who had forwarded texts—or who had been part of Sunita's original group text—had something to add, and I found myself sitting on my bed, looking at people's Pegasus posts on 6A's message board instead of unbraiding my hair. I had to get to school and find out the latest.

I bolted to my feet, hair one half fuzzy, the other half smoothed. I clutched my comb. It was 7:15. I was running behind for the early bus. I needed to hurry.

Rushed, I darted into the kitchen and made my slice of toast and scrambled eggs into an open-faced sandwich. I ate it standing over the sink, getting crumbs everywhere.

"Watch it, Jelly-Beana," Fallon exclaimed, as racing away, I bumped the table, almost knocking over her hot chocolate.

"Don't call me Beana, Flea," I yelled over my shoulder.

"Well, then don't knock over the table, *Beana*," Fallon shot back, sounding cranky.

"Girls, stop bickering. Serena, where's the fire?" Mom asked as I rushed down the hall to flick off the crumbs and brush my teeth.

"I'm trying to catch the early bus." I galloped into

my room and hopped on one foot, pulling on my tennis shoe.

"I can take you to school, I don't have to go in today," Mom said. As I ran back to the bathroom to tie up my hair and put on some lip gloss, my mother followed, frowning slightly.

"Rena, slow down. If you're worried about JC, why don't we just call the house?"

"I—no, no," I shook my head. I hadn't talked to JC since our dinner at her house, which had been forever ago. "I can't just *ask* now."

"I can call," Mom offered. "They don't have to know it's you."

I scowled and shook my head, zipping up my hoodie. I ducked around her to grab my backpack. "You don't understand."

"Serena." Mom slowed my roll through the hallway by standing directly in front of me with crossed arms. I bounced off of her and stumbled over my own feet.

"Mom!"

Mom's whip-sharp voice smacked against my ears. "Serena Estelle. If there's something I don't understand, then you use your words and *help* me understand, thank you. There is entirely too much racing around going on, and not enough explanation. Where are you running off to like a chicken with its head cut off? And why can't you wait on your sister and me?"

I sucked in a huge breath, tears stinging my eyes. "They didn't tell me, okay? I've been JC's best friend since fourth grade, and she's back in the hospital and *no one told me*, Mom. I'm the last person to know."

"I didn't know," Fallon yelled from the kitchen.

"The last person who *matters*," I shouted back, fists clenched.

"So they didn't tell you." Mom's quiet voice pulled my attention back to her. "So what? That means you have to go to school early and do what? Find out more? Listen to more gossip when you could get the news from the source? What? What are you doing, Serena mine?"

"I don't know, okay? I'm just doing whatever!" I almost burst with frustration. "I just want to see if anyone else knows anything. I don't need my *mom* in my face trying to fix it!"

At each shrieked word, my mother's eyes narrowed further, and for a moment, she squinted hard at me, as if studying someone unfamiliar. Then she stalked off, shaking her head.

As soon as she was gone, all my urgency evaporated into confusion. Was she taking me to school, or was she too mad now? Was I in trouble? Had I hurt her feelings? Dropping my bag on the floor, I walked gingerly down the hall and tapped on the wall next to her open bedroom door. "Mama?"

"What, Serena?"

Her voice was as mommish as ever: flat, calm, and uninflected. Braver, I inched through the doorway. Mom was sitting on her bed, holding her phone. She raised her eyebrows, questioning. "What now?"

"Are you calling?" I asked, suddenly breathless.

My mother rolled her eyes, then straightened. "Hello, Sita? Oh, Julia! My goodness, you sound just like your auntie! This is Nova St. John, Fallon and Serena's mom. Uh-huh. Yes, we just wanted to check in and see if you all needed anything, and to see how JC's doing this morning. Okay. Uh-huh, she is? That's good to hear. Oof. I'll bet. Yeah, that sometimes happens. Organ transplants are no joke. Okay, I'll check back later this morning when your auntie Teresita is home. Uh-huh. Okay. You too, Julia. Have a good day."

By the time Mom was finished speaking, I was sitting next to her on the bed, straining to hear the other side of the conversation. When she swiped her phone to end the call and tucked it into her back pocket, I waited for information. Instead, my mother picked up a nail file off of her bedside table. She started filing her nails. The slow, gritty sound of her manicure dug down into my nerves.

"Mom."

"Mmm?"

"Mom!" I threw up my hands. "What did she say?"

Wide-eyed, my mother put her hand to her chest and reared back, faking surprise. "Oh! Well, Serena mine, I don't know if I can just *tell* you. That might put your mom in your face, 'fixing' something for you, and you're just too grown up for that now, aren't you?"

I squirmed, shame making me uncomfortable and warm. "I'm sorry I was rude, Mom," I apologized. "I didn't mean what I said. Thank you for calling. I just feel stupid that nobody told me. It's like *everyone* knows about JC's life now, but I'm the only one she's not talking to."

Mom bumped my shoulder with hers. "If it helps, she's probably not talking to anyone right now. Her cousin says JC's pretty angry that she's been admitted to the hospital. I think she thought she was all done with that."

I wilted against Mom's side. "I thought she was done with that too. Last time, she was there for almost a month."

Mom tucked me under her arm. "It takes as long as it takes, Rena-Beana-Belle. She's going to be on IV medications for a while until that virus is under control. The best thing JC can do for herself is to take her meds and take it easy. You only get in trouble when you forget you're not invincible."

"Well, *I'm* strong and I'm invincible too," Fallon announced from the doorway. "I'm also going to be late for homeroom. Are you driving us, Mom?"

"I'm coming, I'm coming," Mom grumped good-naturedly. "Keep your wig on, Sis."

"This glory is too magnificent for a mere wig," Fallon said, gesturing at her crown of braids. "I call shotgun!" she added.

I rolled my eyes. "Why, God?" I groaned, picking up my backpack. "Why did I get *this* sister? Didn't you have any others?"

"And why did I get both the Drama Divas?" Mom added toward the sky as we got into the car. "Didn't you have any other girls on the shelf that week, God?"

"You wouldn't have me any other way," Fallon said, flouncing into her seat belt.

"Drama Diva?" I scowled. "I'm not dramatic."

Mom turned and gave me a disbelieving stare. Then she burst out laughing. It was kind of annoying. She kept looking at me and snickering all the way to school.

Sometimes she is *so* wrong.

↶22↷

Fear of Friending

"MOM, PROMISE ME. WE'RE only staying five minutes, okay? Mom?"

The pediatric unit of Arden Hospital had yellow and green paint and contrasting floor tiles in swirls of blue, pink, and cream. It was meant to be cheerful. All it did was make me queasy. Here we were—Fallon, reading her phone, Mom carrying the gift bag with the helium balloon bobbing above her in short jerks, and me, dragging my feet behind them as we made our way to the nurses' station. I knew I was pouting, but right now it felt *necessary*. Mom needed to understand that I was almost twelve. I didn't need anyone to make me a play-date—especially not with an ex–best friend who might not even want to see me.

Mom's smile was professional strength. "Hello, we're looking for Gerardo, Room 348?"

"Down to your left," the nurse said, pointing helpfully down the hallway. "See the door with the cart in front of it? It's a couple rooms down after that."

Fallon slowed down so she could look at the scowling birds on the nurse's scrubs, then glared down at me as I pulled on her arm, hurrying her down the hallway. "Stop grabbing me, Beana," she hissed, digging in her heels and coming to a halt. "What is wrong with you?"

"Girls! Get a move on!" Mom whispered from farther down the hall.

"Nothing's wrong," I muttered, crossing my arms. "I just want to get this over with. Mom should have come by herself."

"That's stupid," Fallon argued, walking quickly. "You and JC have been friends since you were, what, seven? Just because you're not *best* friends anymore doesn't mean you act like you don't know her when she's sick."

"I *know* that," I grumbled. "I'm not acting like I don't know her."

"Really? Then maybe try being less of a pill. Don't

be a jerk because you're scared."

I gaped at her, outraged. "I am *not* scared!"

Fallon rolled her eyes and went back to her phone. "What*ever*, Serena."

I stalked on in silence, glaring at the stupid tile. My chest felt tight, and there was a prickly feeling in my throat. Every step closer to where my mother waited impatiently was like walking through glue. My feet slowed, and it got harder and harder to breathe.

Somewhere in my brain a great big gong rang when I hit on the truth. All those panicky, angry feelings I had about this wasn't because I was mad at Mom for making me a playdate like I was a Little or something. This was something else.

Like Fallon said, I was scared of going to see my ex–best friend.

I was scared that JC would look toward the door, expecting someone she liked, like Lani, and be disappointed.

I was scared that JC would ask why I was there.

I was scared that nothing I wanted to tell her— that I was almost ready to upload my first vlog, that Mom had let me get temporary purple hair color at the mall—was going to be interesting to her.

I was scared that all the mean things I had thought

about JC were things she'd thought about *me*.

By the time I got to Mom, my mouth was dry, and I felt like I was choking.

"Listen, you two, whatever's started this round of squabbling, both of you put a lid on it *now*," Mom ordered in an undertone. Then she put her smile on again and knocked on the door. "Sita? JC? Anyone home?"

"Nova! Girls! Oh, so nice that you came all this way," Mrs. Gerardo said, standing from a chair beside the bed as we gathered in the doorway. Seated around the bed were relatives of Mrs. Gerardo's I'd met once before, a sharp-chinned older woman with a rosary and a cane, and a middle-aged man with a priest's collar. They greeted us politely, and I remembered the respectful way JC had pressed her forehead to the older woman's hand.

"Nothing is too far for friends," Mom was saying as she gave Mrs. Gerardo a squeeze. "Is there anything I can do for you while I'm here?"

"Oh, we're fine, we're fine," Mrs. Gerardo began, gesturing toward the door. "Girls, are you hungry? There are butter cookies in that box right there. Jojo, Mommy's going to walk *Tiya* Rosalia to the elevator, all right?"

"I'll give you ladies a moment to talk to your friend," the priest said kindly, and bent over the bed for a moment to lay what looked like a playing card on the bed next to JC's hand.

"Thank you for coming, Father Efren," Mrs. Gerardo said as he turned toward her.

As Mom and Mrs. Gerardo stepped outside, probably so Mrs. G could dish about JC without her hearing, I cleared my throat and looked around the room. There were plastic containers of food, teddy bears, and flowers everywhere. On the wall was taped a larger version of JC's prayer card, with a long-haired Jesus holding out his hands. A red heart glowed on his chest like a tiny sun. JC lay in a ball on her side, turned away from all of us. She wasn't sleeping, though; I saw her shoulders rise and fall on a big sigh.

"You awake, JC?" Fallon asked, poking her foot.

"Nope," JC the smart aleck said.

Fallon raised her eyebrows. When I didn't say anything, she tucked her hands in her armpits and flapped them. *Chicken*, she mouthed.

"Hey, JC, we brought you something," I blurted, trying not to sound nervous.

"Thanks," JC said, but she still didn't turn over.

I looked at Fallon, who shrugged. I shrugged back. Was this why Mom said we needed to cheer her up? I suddenly remembered something and moved closer to the bed. "Ooh, ooh, ooh—JC, did you hear, Mr. Van and Mr. Hutton are adopting a little girl from Ukraine or somewhere?"

JC turned her head a little. "What? No. When did you hear that?"

"Erik called a class meeting and told us we're having a baby shower. Mrs. Bowers told him about the new baby this morning, and said if we were having a shower, she'd help. It's supposed to be a surprise, and we're getting them a gift card from Stork Affair."

"Nice," JC said, blinking slowly. She rubbed her face, leaning back against her pillows.

"Is anything . . . um, hurting you?" I asked, carefully *not* looking at the tape in the bend of her arm, which was holding down a Y-shaped tube that led to a couple of clear medical bags that hung from a metal T-shaped hanger above the bed. I rubbed my arms to keep down the goose bumps. The fat plastic tube was connected to an invisible needle *just stuck right there* in her *arm*. Yeesh.

JC shrugged again and pulled up her knees. "I'm fine."

Fallon tucked her phone away and leaned toward JC's bed. "Not that it's any of my business, but what happened?" she asked in her usual nosy way. "Why are you back here if you're fine? Did something infect the kidney or what?"

JC sighed and turned over again. "The kidney's okay. I . . . don't want to talk about it."

Fallon shrugged. "Fair enough," she said, and plopped down on the window seat. She drummed her fingers on her knee, then pulled her phone out again.

I sighed. Well, that was all the help I was going to get from Fallon. I wracked my brain for a topic, wondering why it was so hard. What would I normally say, if JC weren't acting so weird?

"It's a nice room," I said, looking around. "It's tiny, but at least you don't have to share." Made up of a counter along the wall, a bathroom tucked into a corner, a wide window and window seat beneath it, the room was small but bright. Even though the view through the big window was over the parking lot, there was a pretty evergreen tree fluttering with tiny, busy birds to watch.

"I hate it," JC muttered, her voice filled with loathing.

She was finally looking at me, her usually smooth tan skin looking pale and dry. JC spoke in a loud whisper. "I hate this room. I hate this place. I hate everything. I want to go home, but Mom and the doctor are making me stay here."

I pointed to the IV stand, my own voice dropping to a whisper. "Don't you kind of have to stay here? I mean . . ."

JC made an impatient noise. "No, and it's stupid. I was fine, but I hate how this one pill makes me feel, so I kind of skipped it sometimes. Not all the time, but just . . . some. When they did my bloodwork when I wasn't feeling well, the doctor asked me if I'd skipped anything, and . . . I didn't lie, because she already knew, but Mom dropped a brick. And now she won't let—"

"Wait—what? You stopped taking your meds? You're lucky you didn't *die*, JC!"

JC glowered. "It's not a big deal. It wasn't all my meds, it was *one* pill, *sometimes*. You don't always have to follow every single rule."

Wide-eyed, I stared back, my whisper entirely gone. "Uh, excuse me, when they cut open practically your whole body and take something out, yeah, you *do*! This is totally a big deal! What if something bad happened to the kidney because of that? Then what?" I rubbed my arms, my eyes straying to the bandages on JC's. "I can't believe you!"

JC sighed. "I know," she muttered. "Everybody's already yelled at me."

"I'm not yelling," I said immediately, dropping my voice to make sure. "It's just . . ." I picked my words carefully. "You were my best friend for a long time, and I've known you since forever. It's not like I don't care what happens to you still."

JC looked away, seeming to feel awkward, and my eyes burned. What I'd said—that we weren't best friends anymore—sounded final, and she didn't say anything.

She didn't say I was wrong.

"Oh, that's really sweet, Rena," JC said, her voice wavering. She paused. "I wish—"

"Are you just about ready, girls?" Mom asked, poking her head back into the room. "Mrs. Gerardo is getting another cup of coffee, but then we need to wrap this up, all right? Don't you have a math quiz this week, Serena?"

Frustration screamed from inside of me. I looked from Mom to JC, my heart pounding. *What do you wish? What do you wish? TELL ME*, I wanted to insist, but the moment was gone. JC just fake-smiled, saying, "Thanks for coming," in a polite and completely different voice.

Disappointed, I could hardly smile back. "Don't let your mom eat all your chocolate."

JC shrugged like she didn't care, and I stared. The little peanutty chocolates were her thing. How could she not care about her mom eating all her chocolate? She must feel *really* terrible . . . but if she wouldn't tell me about it, there wasn't much I could do.

I had almost reached the door when I heard, "I'm sorry."

Sorry for what? Not taking her meds? Not being friendlier? For not caring about chocolate? When I turned back, JC had pulled the covers up over her head and lay like a silent rock again.

"I'm sorry too," I said quietly. "I wish you felt better."

Inside, I wished a thousand other things too. But maybe it was too late for wishes.

I closed the door.

SERENA|SAYS

What's up, World? I'm Serena St. John, host of *Serena Says*, vlogging on Fal's Fotography channel! Just FYI, Fal is my sister, and this is my first official vlog—and you're my first official viewers! Welcome to *Serena Says*, and welcome to my DIY segment!

Have you ever had a look through your art supplies and wondered what to do with the bottom half of a pair of jeans, an old metal hanger, or the two bird cookie cutters your mom just bought? Well, I hadn't, either, until tonight! Aaaaand . . .

Right, I know all this stuff isn't all going to work for one project. I mean, obviously. I honestly don't know what I'm going to do with these cookie cutters, but now that Mom's bought them, even though they were only, like, three bucks, I kind of have to use them.

I know, right? Sugar cookies? What was she even thinking? They always look so cool on the Artistly website, but sugar cookies never turn out like the pictures; frosting cookies is super messy. Or else I'm not a good enough artist. Which is probably why this DIY segment is kind of a bad idea . . . but anyway! At *Serena Says*, we'll try anything once!

The WinterFest theme is birds, except for owls, since

somebody else called dibs. Maybe I could sew tiny bird pillows out of the jeans or something. Or little chickens, or . . . ooh, Three French Hens, like the song. I can totally cut out little chicken shapes, sew them together, stuff some tissue paper in them so they're kind of fat, and sew a ribbon on the top, and—done. All I have to do is find some black fabric to make tiny little berets and then everyone will know they're French! That's so cute! French hens! I'm such a genius!

[mad scientist giggling]

Oh, wait, though. That doesn't use the stupid cookie cutters. Dang it!

Well, DIY is all about doing it yourselves, right? There's no crying in crafting, people. We'll just make something else! We'll make . . . basically anything but sugar cookies.

Sugar cookies! I cannot believe my mother. Did she forget the time in kindergarten we made gingerbread houses, and mine got all wet and kind of melted because I kept washing my hands? Did she forget that I hate frosting? It gets everywhere. If I could, like, paint the cookies, it'd be fine. Paint is not sticky. Well, not that sticky. If I could even just use food coloring to color the designs, that would be great. Maybe I could paint crackers? Or . . . hmm. Bibi let us paint cookies once . . . but they were salt dough. Those suckers were heavy, though, so if I make salt dough, I'm going to have to roll them super thin . . . oh, and, boom. I'll use the cookie cutters! Maybe I can find some old rubber stamps to print designs on the birds or something so they're not so boring. I'll paint them. Without frosting, thankyouverymuch.

Um . . . I guess I could use the wire to make them napkin holders or something? Can I glue wire onto dough, though? With a hot glue gun, I guess . . . or maybe I can just glue them to a ribbon or something? Or, ugh, if it came down to it, I guess I could make refrigerator magnets.

Yeah, hard pass on THAT.

Anyway! What about you? What would YOU do with these awesome cookie cutters? Do you like frosting cookies? What's a DIY last-minute art project you've made out of random stuff around the house? I hope you liked this vlog. If you did, go to Fal's Fotography and leave me a note on the Community tab and let me know. Don't forget to subscribe to Fal's Fotography if you want to hear more from me.

Serena says let your genius flag fly! And have fun!

That's my story, and I'm out.

Aaaand . . . that was okay. Not, like, exceptionally perfect, but okay.

And I need to start taking chances at some point,

sooo . . . So that's it. I'm doing it. I'm uploading.

Oh, this is *so* scary. But whatever, right? I'm doing it . . . . Ready, set . . . NOW.

It's loading . . . and . . . done.

Now I want to bury the computer in a hole somewhere. AAAH!!!! I'm so nervous.

23

A Kitchen Witch

"WHATCHA DOIN'?" FALLON'S VOICE was muffled where it found me, head and shoulders deep in the linen closet. Stretching for the top shelf, I stood on a box on top of a kitchen chair.

"What's it look like?" I muttered, wobbling as I turned.

I'd been running around since I'd gotten home. Mr. Van had told us we only had fourteen school days left before Thanksgiving break, the discovery of which made me cranky and panicky all at once. After all my work on our Nile Crescent project, I'd fallen way behind on WinterFest—now only SIX-TEEN days away—and I was starting to panic. It wasn't like I would fail sixth grade if I didn't bring something for a raffle basket. Citizenship grades weren't exactly real grades, but the basket was also part of being in Brigid Ogan's student body—about having school spirit. Especially now that I was kind of a group leader, I couldn't let 6A down.

"Pfft—I don't actually *care* what you're doing. I was just being polite because I have *manners*." Fallon's lofty tone made me roll my eyes. Then I narrowed them when I realized she was still standing behind me.

"Wait, you don't have manners. You want something, don't you?" I frowned. "What?"

Fallon bounced on her toes. "Serena, why can't you—never mind. I just need to borrow, like, seven dollars until I get paid for babysitting the Weeks' kid this weekend. And I know you still have last year's birthday money from Bibi."

"Well, I have it because I'm *saving it*," I reminded my sister.

"I know, but I'll pay you back on Saturday. Jeez, Serena, it's two freaking days."

"Technically three," I said, then shrugged at her expression. "What? On the Roman calendar, day starts at midnight, right? It's not midnight Thursday yet."

Fallon's eyes narrowed to slits. "*Serena.* Can I borrow ten bucks, or what?"

"Wasn't it seven?" I wondered, then held up my hands as she lunged. "Don't kill me!" I squealed, ducking away, then screamed in earnest. I'd forgotten about my standing-on-a-chair-on-a-box thing.

After more screaming, crashing against the wall, knocking off a picture, and landing on my sister—who, I admit, mostly tried to catch me—it was quiet. With a lot of jabbing elbows and knees, we got ourselves up. I rubbed my aching butt as Fallon set the chair upright again.

"Sorry," she said a little breathlessly. "I didn't think you'd actually fall."

I flexed my shoulder. "Eh, it's fine. I should have just gotten the stepstool." I rubbed my backside again. "So what's the ten bucks for?"

My sister brightened. "A new lens! There's one kit for phones, and you can take super-detailed close-up pictures with one lens or use a fish-eye lens and take panoramas. Cool, huh?"

"I guess," I said. Fallon's camera addiction was well documented. "Is it for yearbook?"

"Well, kind of." Fallon shrugged. "It's mostly for me. I saw this picture of a fruit fly on the internet, and I wanted to see if I could shoot a close-up like that. Mrs. Vejar's got these little flower flies in a tank, and I want to find out if they're hairy like the fruit flies or what."

Eew. "Um, sounds great," I said with a weak smile.

Fallon snorted. "Oh my gosh, Serena, your pants are *burning.*"

"What?" I jumped away from the hallway heater—which wasn't even on—patting down my legs. Then I rolled my eyes. Right. *Liar, liar, pants on fire.* My sister was *so* weird. "Whatever, Flea," I said, and turned toward my room. "Come take my money and get out."

"What was it you were looking for, anyway?" Fallon asked again as I dug into my glittery blue metal cashbox for the requested loan.

"Our stamping kits. Remember that one year when Mom made us make an anniversary card for Bibi and Poppy? And we bought a lot of rubber stamps of flowers and stars and stuff?"

"Oh yeah! Those are in the top of my closet," Fallon told me. "I'll get them."

In the kitchen, I pulled out my ingredients, grimacing guiltily at Mom's fancy cake flour. Despite what I'd said on the vlog I'd uploaded, I wasn't quite as sure about making salt dough as I'd been earlier—Mom might be really cranky about me wasting food, so I needed to make this quick and get out of the kitchen. Unfortunately, after lining up my ingredients, I discovered one more problem—we didn't have nearly enough salt for the two cups I needed for salt dough.

I thumped my head on the table in frustration. "Aaaargh!" I groaned. "Why couldn't this be easy?" Sighing, I opened my eyes and looked sideways at the box of cornstarch. Absentmindedly, I scanned the small print on its side . . . then I stood up and read the recipe right-side up. "Cornstarch clay?" I now had a Plan B. I only hoped it would work as well as Plan A.

One cup of cornstarch, plus two cups of the baking soda beneath the bathroom sink, mixed together in a pot with a cup and a drizzle of water, and . . . it looked like thick milk. Was this going to work? Frowning, I put the pot on the stove.

Stirring the mix over a low flame, I could hear Fallon talking on the phone—again—about her camera lens, and what she was going to do with it. Since she was kind of squealing, I knew she was talking to Sharyn. While Fallon liked bugs, Sharyn was obsessed with taking pictures of buildings. They were well matched as best friends.

I didn't get squealy about pictures of buildings or bugs. I didn't love dance, like Julia and Sunita, or adore video games, like Eliana—or my briefcase, like Harrison, or *Modern Divas*, or sports, or anything other people in my class did. I wondered if I was too boring. Mr. Baumgartner always said that in history, great people had great passion. I wasn't *passionate* about anything, exactly, but I loved doing things like making crafts or being on camera for my vlog. Maybe it was just that the word "passionate" sounded too . . . big, and too emo. Maybe I was just a great person who was going to have great passion without squealing. I could live with that.

While I hadn't been paying attention, the white mixture had changed from watery white to a goo that clung to the spoon and pulled away from the sides of the pot. My sister, still on the phone, popped into the kitchen to grab an ice cream sandwich from the freezer. She peered nosily into the pot as she unwrapped it. "Add milk. Mashed potatoes need more liquid than that," she instructed, then snatched the spoon and blew on it quickly before moving it toward her mouth.

"No, don't eat—!"

"BLAAAAAAAAH!" Fallon gagged and spit out the mouthful of clay into the sink.

Over the loud sound of her spitting, I giggled. "I told you, it's not edible! Sorry!" As my sister gargled, I picked up the spoon and rescued the ice cream sandwich from the splashes in the sink.

"Ugh," Fallon panted, rinsing her mouth under the sink tap. "No, not you," she said into the phone, blinking watery eyes as she wiped her mouth with a dish towel, then snatched her ice cream from my hands. "My sister's trying to kill me with her cooking!"

"Nobody asked you to eat it," I said, but Fallon had huffed away down the hall.

I dumped the hot clay on the cutting board and got out a rolling pin. When it had cooled a bit, the cornstarch blend, warm and silky-smooth, felt *way* better than Bibi's salt dough, which left my hands crusty and dry. Now all I needed was for it to make good, strong birds.

"Here goes nothing," I muttered.

The clay rolled out easily into a thin sheet, and I hesitated over my choice of rubber stamps and cookie cutters. One of them was a chicken or a duck, but another one could maybe be an owl . . . which reminded me of Lani and JC's magnets. I wondered how JC felt. The last time I'd called the hospital, Mrs. Gerardo told me Lani was there. Maybe they were working on their project too. Or planning JC's birthday party. Maybe they'd decided not to invite me . . .

"Knock it off," I muttered, resisting the weight of the sad feelings. "Think of something else."

For 6A's bird baskets, Eliana was making chicken empanadas scalloped in the shape of wings—well, mostly her mom was, but Eli was helping. I wondered what Harrison would do, make little briefcases with wings? I cracked a tiny grin.

An hour later, and my mood was much better. I'd had to make the ornaments thicker than I expected—I couldn't get the thinner rolled ornaments off the cutting board. When I'd gotten bored with one shape, I'd gently pulled on the cheap metal cutters to make some a little larger, so I had fat birds and smaller birds with slightly different tails. For a few, I'd used ink on my stamp pad, and I hoped the colors wouldn't fade too much as the ornaments dried.

"So you made soaps?" Fallon, still nosy, but wary now, peeked into the room. "Out of potatoes?"

"I told you—it's not potatoes and it's not soap. It's cornstarch clay."

"I didn't know cornstarch made clay." Fallon peered over my shoulder. "Oh, pretty!"

When I hadn't left the ornaments white, I'd stamped with a design made with a dark-blue ink to make a nice wintry blue and white, instead of Christmas red and green. Even without their berets, my French hens were looking fancy.

"How did you make the ribbon holes?" Fallon asked, eyeing the neat circles.

"I wiggled around a piece of spaghetti," I said. "Toothpicks were too small. I'm going to hot glue hairbands to some of them after I sand them and seal them—people can use them for napkin rings or for regular hairbands."

"French hen hairbands!" Fallon asked. "That is so random. I want one!"

I looked proudly at my birds. They needed to dry overnight—or oven bake for an hour watched closely—but I was done for now. Mom would be home soon, and it was time to clean up the kitchen, plus I was starving.

"This is much cooler than a birdbath," Fallon said, trailing a finger over a pattern of shooting stars that made wings and feathers on one bird. "NO ONE is going to top this, Serena."

I shrugged, my smile a little shy. "Fal, I copied it from Artistly. Tons of people have already made them."

"I know, but I mean nobody at Brigid Ogan, and none exactly like these," Fallon insisted. She gently punched my shoulder. "This is cool. I like."

"Even though I tried to kill you?" I teased.

"You tried," Fallon said, her eyes narrow in mock warning. "But I'm on to you now. Don't cook. Just keep making chicken hairbands."

The warm feeling Fallon's words gave me stayed as I put things away. When I heard Mom's key in the door, the feeling lit up brighter as Fallon called, "Mom! Hey, Mom, come here! Look what Serena made!"

I couldn't help the smile on my face. I felt like I could have thought up another fifty cool projects without even breaking a sweat.

SERENA|SAYS

FAL'S FOTOGRAPHY

184 subscribers

HIGHLIGHTED POST: Fal in Focus 1 week ago

Welcome to the Community tab for Fal's Fotography! Did you see my sister's vlog, *Serena Says*? Thank you for watching! Check out these pics of Serena's finished DIY project! I like the blue-and-white bands the best.

What would you like to see next in her DIY series? Don't forget to subscribe and stay tuned for more from both of us! —Fal

Laura Scheingart, 2 days ago

Aww, cute! Your sister is good at this.

Ally Leonard, 2 days ago

LOVE THE CHICKENS

VantheMan, 3 days ago

Nice camera presence, Serena. Some good progress!

ElianaBanana, 6 days ago

SUPER cute, Ree! Me likey.

SlideshowSharyn, 7 days ago

Nice job, chick.

24

Like a Boss

"CAMERON JONES, MY OFFICE, please."

"Oh no," Ally whispered, looking up from her outline. "There goes our A."

After the loud burst of laughter from the computer corner, Ms. Pettinelli's usually sunny face was stern and serious. Our whole group watched as Mr. Van followed Cam and the librarian into the small room and tilted the blinds for privacy.

"Dang it, Cameron," I muttered. Mr. Van stood in the doorway with his arms crossed, keeping a stern eye on the rest of the class while taking part in Cameron's meeting. This was the third time Ms. Pettinelli had said something to Cameron today, and now that Mr. Van was involved, Cam was in twice as much trouble.

"I wish we could kick him out of our group," Lani grumped. "It's not fair that we're all working so hard and he's not doing *anything*."

"Cameron's working," Mateo immediately defended his friend.

"Sure, he just . . . took a side-trip from getting his colored pencils?" I shook my head as Mateo shrugged. "Come on, Mateo. Even you told him he was going to get in trouble."

"Man." Eliana sighed. "I wish we could do something."

"About Cameron?" Ally gave Eliana a frown.

"No, silly, about our *grade*." Eliana giggled, then looked toward Ms. Pettinelli's office. "I mean, it's not fair that Cameron can ruin the grade for the whole group. Not that he's going to," Eliana added, because she's a super-nice person. "I just don't think *anyone* should have that power."

"I know," I agreed glumly. Lani nodded.

"Can't you go talk to Ms. Pettinelli?" Mateo asked. "Teachers always like girls."

I scowled. "That's sexist discrimination. Teachers like *people*—boys and girls—who do their *work*.

Since that's what you've been doing, why don't *you* talk to her?"

"Well, you are our group leader," Lani pointed out, sounding way too reasonable.

Dang. I looked around the circle. Ally looked hopeful. Mateo looked demanding. Lani looked . . . like she always did, like she was waiting for me to do something interesting so she could watch. Eliana leaned back in her wheelchair and grinned. She knew I didn't want to go.

That little grin got on my nerves. "Fine." I pushed back my chair. "Okay. I'll talk to Ms. Pettinelli. But . . . don't expect anything, people. They already made up the rules and wrote them down and made copies for all of sixth grade. They're not gonna change them just for me."

"They might." Ally was an optimist.

"They'd better," Mateo said with a serious frown.

Gripping my mechanical pencil in my fist, I . . . turned around and looked longingly back at the safety of my group. Ally and Mateo were looking at their work, but Lani was watching, still looking interested. Eliana smirked, and I stuck out my tongue. Reluctantly, I dragged myself to the dragon's lair . . . Ms. Pettinelli's office.

I hesitated as I came to the door. Mr. Van had his back to me. Should I say "knock, knock," or should I wait for them to get done with Cameron? Would Mr. Van be mad I was asking about my grades? Sometimes he got tired of people asking for things like extra credit and stuff. He could be tricky.

I cleared my throat, and Mr. Van turned. Cameron looked up, then at the floor. He didn't look happy.

"Um, Mr. Van?" my voice cracked.

Mr. Van put on a pleasant expression. "What can I help you with, Serena?"

I curled my toes in my shoes. "Is now a good time to talk to you about working in groups?" I asked.

Mr. Van sighed. "Cameron, go back to your seat, please. I'll talk with you later." Mr. Van turned back to me and lowered his voice. "Serena, if you're here to ask if I'll put Cameron in someone else's group, I've told everyone already, the groups are going to stay as—"

"That's not what I meant," I interrupted, then winced. "Sorry," I added quickly. The easiest way to annoy Mom was interrupting.

Mr. Van raised his eyebrows. "What did you want

to say about groups, then?" he asked.

"Can I talk to you and Ms. Pettinelli at the same time?" I asked, looking into the office.

Ms. Pettinelli waved me in. "What's going on, Serena?" she asked, her usual warm smile back where it belonged.

I thought fast. Mr. Van didn't want to move anyone around in groups, and he didn't like it when we complained. So, without complaining, and without asking for anything for myself, what could I do about Cameron? Was this one of Mrs. Henry's opportunities to stand up and speak out? I stood a little straighter.

"I'm here as student advocate for Cameron Jones," I began.

Ms. Pettinelli's brown eyes went wide. "Really!" she said. She looked at Mr. Van. "Is this something that you do in 6A?"

"Uh, no," Mr. Van said, looking startled. "Tell us what you mean, Serena."

Last night, Mom had been on the phone with one of the patient advocates at New Vista, working out something a patient needed. Patient advocates helped patients get what they needed. A student advocate could do the same thing.

"Cameron needs help, and since he's in our group, my group, um, asked me to help him," I said, feeling my way forward. "We want him to get a good grade on our group project—and we want a good grade, too, so I want to ask you for, um, an extra project, just for Cameron."

Mr. Van looked confused. "What?"

"I'll help him with it," I said quickly. "He's my responsibility."

"Wait, wait, wait just a minute here," Ms. Pettinelli said, holding up a hand. "Cameron Jones is *not* your responsibility, Serena. Everyone makes choices to stay on task—your choices are your only responsibility."

"Well, I just thought, because I'm his group leader . . ." I turned toward Mr. Van. "I was hoping you could give him an extra assignment so he could make up the points he lost by getting in trouble. Maybe he could earn our group those points back?"

"Ah." Ms. Pettinelli made a little face and sat back in her chair. "I understand now."

Mr. Van sighed. "Um, thank you, Serena. Why don't you go back to your seat now, and I'll, uh, get back to you on this advocate thing, all right?"

I hesitated. "You won't forget?"

Mr. Van smiled so big that wrinkles fanned out from the corners of his greenish-brown eyes. "Nope. I'll remember this all day, Serena St. John."

"Um, okay," I said, giving Mr. Van a worried look. *That* didn't sound too good.

"Well?" Mateo asked in a low voice as I slid back in my seat.

I shot a glance over my shoulder. Mr. Van was walking around one side of the room, while Ms. Pettinelli stood in the doorway to her office, watching everyone work.

"Not now," I whispered. "Everyone get busy."

Five heads bent over their papers and five pencils and pens moved.

Mr. Van paused by our table. "Looking good over here. Serena, may I have a word?"

I gulped.

"I have another assignment!" Cameron bleated. "Why'd you ask him for *that*?"

"He can earn the group our lost points back? YES!" Lani high-fived Ally, looking gleeful.

"I'm going to help you," I reminded Cameron, who looked like he'd been hit with a stick.

"We're *all* going to help you," Eliana said loyally.

"We're your group, Cam. We just want our A."

"I knew you'd talk him into it," Mateo said.

"You did?" I blurted. "I didn't!"

"I can't believe I have another assignment," Cameron groaned pitifully. "My life bites."

"It's your own fault," Lani reminded him. "You messed around all day."

"What does he have to do?" Eliana asked.

"He has to design a giant Egyptology Exhibit poster for the third graders," I explained. "Ms. Pettinelli will display it on WinterFest night with the rest of our Egypt projects."

"What? That's all? That's easy," Cameron said, relief coloring his voice. "I can do that."

"I *know* you can do that," I told him, exasperated. "That's why I asked Mr. Van if you could. Just don't screw up after this, okay? Mr. Van said this is your *one* chance."

"I won't screw up, boss," said Cameron eagerly. He dug in his bag and produced a metal box of graphite pencils and pulled out a fresh pad of drawing paper. "I'm starting now."

"I can't believe you," Eliana marveled as the three-minute bell rang and Mr. Van shooed us out and to our next class. "You got Mr. Van to agree, and Cameron actually worked and didn't talk for, like, ten minutes straight. You're like Super Group Leader, or, wait—you're the Teacher Whisperer. I don't even know how you DID that."

I gave Eliana a smug smile. "Well, I *am* the group leader," I said, but I was mostly joking. As strict as Mr. Van is, everyone knows there's no such thing as a Teacher Whisperer, but whatever. I did a little happy dance down the hall anyway.

SERENA|SAYS

What's up, World? It's your girl Serena! Welcome back to my vlog on Fal's Fotography channel!

First of all, thank you so much for all the comments from my DIY video! I was so scared to upload it, and now . . . since you liked my DIY, I'm going to do more, and upload a book vlog and other stuff, so stay tuned for that.

Second of all, it is a GREAT day! It's finally cold enough for me to wear my new mermaid tights—and my ankle boots, which I really, really love. Also, it's only two weeks till WinterFest. AND best of all? I got an invitation to a BIRTHDAY PARTY in the mail today! The card is black and has JC's initials—JCSG—on the top in gold. On the next line, in thin gold lettering, it says "our tween" and then "a QUEEN" in huge gold letters on the next line. There's a ton of gold glitter all over the edges, which means there is a ton of gold glitter all over my room, and I don't even care. It is SO cute.

Inside it says: "It's hard to believe in a blink of an eye that 12 years have just flown by! The pleasure of your company is requested on the occasion of Jolynne Christina's birthday." And then she wrote "sleepover!" and "makeovers!" and "movie marathon" in white gel pen across the bottom. It is going to be really, really cool. JC's aunt Gina works on soap opera sets in Southern California, so she always has lots of clothes and makeup, and she's bringing them for us to play with. And since Mr. Gerardo sings all the time, I know there's going to be karaoke, and lots and lots (seriously, a metric ton) of food. It's not going to be as big a party as when JC turned eleven—she can't invite all of the girls in sixth grade because she's not supposed to have a lot of germs around, but it'll still be amazing, and . . .

There! Will! Be . . . **Boys!**

Not when we're sleeping, duh, but before then. It's kind of a big deal? But kind of not—I mean, it's not like we don't see boys every day at school. But still . . . not at sleepovers.

Anyway!

Well, anyway . . . Thanksgiving is coming, and since Mom's on call, Bibi and Poppy are coming over! My uncle Ron is ditching us for his girlfriend's family in Phoenix, but whatever, more food for us.

There are TWELVE SCHOOL DAYS left until Autumn Break, people! I know some people hate Thanksgiving, but I love it, 'cause it's none of the homework and ALL the pie, and ALL the games, plus Bibi and Poppy. What about you? Do you celebrate Thanksgiving or

Friendsgiving? Does your family have holiday hype, or do you do friend-family stuff? Or maybe you don't care at all? Sometimes people hate holidays like Thanksgiving because they're part of a negative history, but to me, they just mean hanging out with people you love—it doesn't have to be more than that, if you don't want it to be.

That's my story, and I'm out.

25

Say Yes to the Mess

"NOW THIS IS CUTE," my grandmother, Bibi, said, pulling out a red plaid jacket with a yellow stripe running through it. She held it up against herself with a little nod. "This could work."

"Poppy wouldn't be caught dead wearing plaid," I said, and laughed at Bibi's scowl.

"No, he wouldn't," my grandmother said, "and it's not cut right for me. Oh well."

She put it back, and I rolled my eyes. Bibi and Poppy, our grandparents, had driven up from Madrone on Friday morning. Poppy had plans to roast a turkey breast and make his special brisket, and Fallon and Bibi had been discussing pies with anticipation. We were signed up to volunteer at the veterans' home for their Thanksgiving dinner, but I couldn't get excited just yet. All I could think about was JC's party that was happening tomorrow night, the party for which Bibi was supposed to be helping me find an outfit.

So far, we'd walked through the whole mall and through the smaller stores that lined the next block. We'd visited eight or nine stores with tween departments since we'd gotten here at eleven, and we'd only bought one adorable bell-shaped gray wool hat. For Bibi.

"What do you say we get a cup of coffee or something, Serena? You can tell me what you want to wear to this party so we can get serious about our shopping."

"I'd tell you what I want if I knew what I wanted," I said, following my grandmother from the store into the brisk and sunny afternoon. "I just want to look . . . different, you know? Not just the same as always."

"Well, you've got all day to come up with different," Bibi said, nodding toward a small bakery on the corner. "We'll catch our breath a minute at the Butter and Bean and then we'll find something, okay?"

The shop smelled like cupcakes and coffee, which

made Bibi certain that we were in the right place. Reading the sign above the counter, I frowned when my phone vibrated. My eyebrows shot up when I saw the number.

"JC?" I blurted. "What's up?"

"Serenaaaaaaa," JC wailed. "Everything is *horrible*."

"Hang on," I said, and tapped Bibi's arm. The "family time" rule applied to the phone, too, and I knew Mom wouldn't like me ignoring Bibi to talk for too long.

Bibi looked back from where she stood ahead of me in line. "Do you need to step out?"

I gave my grandmother an apologetic grimace. "It's an emergency."

Mom had dropped Bibi and me at the mall on her way to work, while Poppy had taken Fallon to the camera store for Christmas shopping. They'd agreed to come get us when they were done, so Bibi and I had taken our time, mostly window-shopping while we hung out. I was surprised to hear from JC. I hadn't really talked to her since I'd RSVP'd to her party invitation.

Bibi waved me away. "Go on ahead outside and talk, Serena. I'll get you hot chocolate. You still like whipped cream? Cinnamon?"

I nodded. "I'll be quick, Bibi," I promised. Pushing through the crowd, I found a cement planter in the sun and sat down, rubbing my arms.

"I'm back," I said, adjusting the phone to my ear. "Tell me everything."

"It's Tatay," JC said, tears in her voice. "He thinks I should wear this *awful* dress."

"Your dad? But I heard you had your dress," I said, watching a red sports car attempting to parallel park in too small of a space.

"I do! And it's gorgeous, and I told you about it, right? It's sleeveless with black netting across the chest, with gold sequins over—"

"Yeah, I heard from Lani," I said hastily, cutting her off before she could describe the sequined top and layers of foofy tulle. I'd also already heard from Mom, who heard it from Mrs. Gerardo how JC couldn't figure out if she should wear her hair up or down, if she should wear her mother's gold sandals or if she should dust glitter on her black sandals, or if her mother's black pearls or the sparkly gold hoops her auntie brought would look best. Mom was the one who suggested JC change accessories halfway through the party—which JC thought was the coolest idea ever. All of JC's friends and family were getting pretty good at unsticking her from party details that kept getting her stuck.

"So there's another dress?" I prompted, when JC paused.

"Well, it's my mother's dress, from when she had her eighteenth birthday coming-out party, and my *lola* brought it over, because she had it in storage for when I have *my* eighteenth birthday, but they don't think it'll fit then, because I'm already bigger than Nanay was at her age, so my lola thought I should wear it now because this is a special birthday, because of the surgery and everything. And Nanay said she was happy to see it, but I didn't have to wear it, but Tatay's trying to make me, because seeing it made Nanay cry, and Serena, it's so, so, so much *lace*! And it's pink—bright pink! And back then, they worked so hard to pay for it, and my lola brought it all this way—"

"Well, can't you just change outfits when you're changing earrings and stuff?" I asked, smiling at a little boy who was solemnly staring, sucking his thumb as his mother led him by. "You can start out wearing it and take a family picture or something, then go upstairs and change."

"Maybe," JC wavered, "but, Rena, pink isn't me,

you know? Plus, Lani's wearing black, too, so . . ." She trailed off.

"Hmm," I said, turning to see where Bibi was in the line. She was almost done, and waiting by the orders counter, so I thought fast. "Well, maybe you can—"

"So, listen, I thought maybe you could wear it," JC blurted in a rush.

"Wait, what? *What?*" I'd been standing to head inside but crashed down onto the planter again as if my legs couldn't hold my weight. "Oh, nuh-uh, JC, not your mom's dress. Why would you think that was a great idea?"

"Because Nanay and Tatay like you," JC said, as if it made the most sense of anything in the world. "My lola likes you too. They'll trust you not to spill anything on it. And then *you* can change out of it after a while."

"JC, it's your mom's eighteenth birthday dress. You said a coming-out party was like a quinceañera, almost like a wedding! That makes that dress, like, a family heirloom or something. Can't Julia wear it? She's at least a relative, and she's closer to eighteen than we are."

"It won't fit," JC said. "Her bottom's too big."

I rolled my eyes. "Well, what makes you think it'll fit me? Your mom's pretty, um, curvy, and if you haven't noticed I'm—"

"We'll pin it and stuff socks down the front if it doesn't fit. Come on, Serena, you can do it for like, an hour, right? Tatay and my lola will be happy, and Nanay will be happy we helped you find a dress."

Everyone would be happy, from the sound of things, but me. "JC, I'm at the mall with Bibi right now, getting an outfit. I don't need—"

"Don't answer right now," JC said. "Just promise me you'll *think* about it, okay? Come over when you're done shopping and try it on. You don't have to even take it home. You can come over, put it on, and take it off, just that fast."

"I—"

"Please, please, *please*, Bestie? It's for my birthday."

Bestie? I wasn't JC's bestie anymore. She was buttering me up with loads of syrup. Had she asked Lani to wear the dress? Did I *want* her to ask Lani? What if *Lani* said yes? Wouldn't I rather be the good friend who helped out?

What if this was the only reason JC had asked me to her party?

I closed my eyes, angry with JC, and frustrated with myself that her pleading words still had the power to make me wish she truly meant them. "I'll think about it, all right? Right now, I have to go— Bibi wants me."

"Thank you, thank you, thank you," JC gushed, and hung up.

Jamming my phone into my pocket, I glared out over the eager lines of holiday shoppers. Sick with my stomach's churning, the idea of super-sweet whipped cream and chocolate made me want to heave.

Mom always says that different doesn't mean bad, but this time I knew: wearing JC's mother's dress was an idea that was really different . . . and also positively, absolutely, definitely, *really* bad.

Maybe this would be the first one of JC's birthday parties I skipped.

∽26∾

Serena Speaks Up

IT WAS HOT UPSTAIRS, hotter than the room full of smiling relatives singing along with the karaoke performers. Downstairs, JC's beaming aunties were busy dishing out massive trays of lumpia and spaghetti, and in the backyard beneath the red and blue Philippine flag with its white triangle and golden sun and stars, something was sending up a plume of savory smoke from the barbecue. Upstairs, there were other, less pleasing smells, mostly of conflicting, flowery perfumes, but also of scorched hair and overheated blow dryers. A few of the older cousins in fancy slippers went in and out of the guest rooms, and I could hear someone singing loudly to a song on their phone.

"Serena! Finally," JC exclaimed when my dragging feet found her adjusting a sparkly gold tiara in her fancy hairdo. "Did you get something to eat? You're so late I thought you weren't coming," she added, then twirled, gesturing. "Isn't this dress amazing? Did you see Lani downstairs? Doesn't her makeup look amazing? Auntie Gina did hers too. Did you see her brothers? Oh, wait, have you been outside yet? There's barbecue. Uncle Paul brought his guitar. We are going to have so much fun!"

"Happy birthday," I said, wiping my hands on the legs of my black pants. To match the gold sequins on the top of her dress, JC wore gold eye shadow and a gold sequined bow in her updo. Compared to me in my silver hoops, the sleeveless white turtleneck Bibi had bought me, and my stretchy black pants, JC looked sparkly—super sparkly—and happier than I'd seen her in a long, long time.

Prickles of dread swept the back of my neck as JC beamed. "It *is* a happy birthday. I've been waiting for this *forever*, and my stomach even feels good today. Come look at what you're wearing." Grabbing my arm, JC towed me down the hall to her parents' room.

"Um, actually . . ." I dug in my heels at the doorway to her parents' room while JC went on alone to the closet and slid open the mirrored doors. "Does your mom know about this?"

JC ignored me and swung a full-skirted pink gown out across her parents' bed. "Tada!"

It was . . . a lot of pink. There was dark-pink embroidered lace on top of a light-pink, scoop-necked dress. There were high, stiff, puffed sleeves made out of lace. Below, the dress pinched in at the knees, and poufed out again with layers and layers and *layers* of floaty pink lace netting. The dress reminded me of an upside-down pink dandelion . . . that had exploded.

"It's . . . um." I blinked. "It's kind of big."

"And there's a little scarf thingy that goes with it." JC dug into the closet again. "See?"

I swallowed. I'd spent last night thinking of all the things that would happen if I wore JC's dress; how her lola would be shocked, how her aunties would whisper behind their hands. Mrs. Gerardo would be maybe surprised, or maybe angry—with me *and* with JC. She'd probably think Mom had never taught me anything, ever, at all, and her feelings might be hurt that JC would lend her special dress to just anyone.

I'd thought for a long while, too, about all the things that might happen if I chose *not* to wear the dress. The worst that could happen was that JC might scream at me and tell me I wasn't welcome at her party if I wouldn't wear the dress. She might tell everyone at Brigid Ogan what a bad friend I was when she came back and make everyone in our class hate me too. That probably wouldn't happen . . . mainly because it seemed sometimes like JC already didn't like me very much. At least our friendship probably couldn't get any *worse*.

JC had said to "just think about it," but I knew what my head was telling me—that I shouldn't be wearing a dress that JC's mom had worked hard to pay for, a long time ago, when her family had no money. I knew what my heart was saying—that I didn't want to wear a dress that I didn't pick, to look a certain way with lace and pink and sequins and scarf thingies that I wasn't sure I wanted to look.

Even though I'd decided to accept whatever consequences came, I still dreaded saying the words. But as JC turned from the closet, I knew it was time to take the opportunity to use my voice. I curled up my fingers into fists and squeezed out the words on all one breath.

"Um, I'm not going to wear your dress, JC, 'kay? Sorry."

JC dropped the scarf on the closet floor and stiffened. "Serena!"

"I didn't promise," I mumbled to the bedspread, unable to hold her furious gaze.

"No, you didn't." JC's words snapped out like brittle pieces of ice. "You *wouldn't* promise. Serena, you're not being a very good best friend—"

"Am I?" I blurted, looking up.

It was supposed to sound sharp and mature, supposed to make JC stop talking and listen. But my voice wobbled and cracked. Instead of sounding womanly, I sounded weepy.

"What? What do you mean 'am I'?" JC demanded. "Is this about the birdbath again?"

"What? No! Yes." I waved my hands. "I thought you and Lani were besties now. I mean . . . you dressed up for Twin Day, JC. And yeah, you did ditch me on the birdbath . . ."

"Can't I have more than one best friend?" JC demanded. "And anyway, that was ages ago, and Twin Day was just for fun. You should have said if you were mad."

Of course, it wasn't *JC's* fault. I scowled. "I am NOT mad!"

"Well then, wear the stupid dress!"

"No! It's your mother's dress, JC! I can't wear it!"

"Well, *I* can't wear it. Nothing I'm wearing goes with it," JC shot back, holding the full skirt against her sparkly sequins. "See? It won't work." She threw the dress on the bed.

"It'll work," I said. "Look, just put on the gold sandals, like you planned, and roll with it. It's kind of . . . old-fashioned, but so what? It's your *mom's special dress*. Wear it for five minutes."

Silently, JC glared, her big brown eyes narrowed and fierce. I glared right back. Maybe last summer that glare would have scared me, but this school year I'd stared down madder people—like Cameron or Mateo when they messed around on our group project, or Mom, when Fallon and I fought. No matter how mad JC was, me wearing Mrs. Gerardo's special coming-out dress wasn't right, and I wouldn't—couldn't—let JC talk me into it. Not this time.

After a long, silent war, JC looked away, shoulders slumped. "I don't *want* to," she whined. "You seriously did not see my mother going on and on and on about this dress. It was for her debut party when they first moved from the Philippines. It took her and my lola a whole year to save up for it. It was the very first fancy party their family had in America. She *cried*, Serena! And it's got all these pleats and this nasty, scratchy fabric, and I hate it! And I'm probably going to spill something on it, and she'll cry some more, and I'll never hear the end of it from the aunties. And I've been sick, and, and it's my *birthday*, Serena. I'm sorry if you think I'm not a good friend, but can't you just help me anyway?"

JC was *finally* starting to really talk to me, even if she was mad. I took a deep breath. "JC, I'm sorry too. I haven't been a good friend, and I'm sorry this seems like I'm not helping. I'll always be your friend. But you know why I can't wear the dress—your lola's here, and all of your aunts and cousins and everybody. Seeing you in your mom's dress is going to make all of them super happy, right? And even though it's all scratchy and gross, the dress is super special to them. Since it's so special, your mom won't mind if you just put it on for five minutes and take it off, right? You'll go and walk around the living room, and I'll be right next to you the whole time. I'll paparazzi you and stuff, and then I'll help you get the other dress back on. You're in, you're out, and your dad's totally proud of you. Come on, JC. You know it'll be better if you wear it."

JC stared at the floor, pouting for another long moment, and then she sighed. "Fine, fine, okay. I just wanted you to wear it so if something happened, it wouldn't all be my fault," JC said, and pulled the black pearl earrings out of her ears. "I was afraid if you didn't wear it, though, Mom would let Julia wear it, and even though I hate it, I'd rather you wear it than her."

I rolled my eyes. She was being honest, at least. "Didn't you say it wouldn't fit her?"

JC sighed and gestured for me to unzip her. "I maybe lied a little. Okay, so while I'm wearing this . . . this hideousness, what are you going to wear? You'll look boring next to me, in just black and white," JC said as she shrugged out of the black and gold dress.

"I'm fine as I am," I said, unzipping the stiff, scratchy, lacy pink dress, and climbing onto the bed. Carefully, I balanced on my knees and helped JC lower the floofy skirts over her stiffly sprayed hair.

"Are you sure?" JC asked, muffled underneath yards of tulle. "You really can borrow a dress or something. Auntie Gina can do your makeup too. You look nice, Serena, but you could borrow something fancy—not this dress, but something cool."

Was I fine? I thought about it. My hands were dry now. My shoulders weren't hunched anymore. All the worst things that *might* have happened weren't happening after all, and best of all, JC and I were back on track—different friends now, but friends all the same.

I smiled at myself in Mrs. Gerardo's mirror, relieved I could recognize the person in the sleeveless white sweater and pretty hoop earrings I saw smiling back at me. "I'm good. I'm positive."

SERENA|SAYS

What's up, World? Back by popular demand, it's your girl Serena. Welcome back to my vlog on Fal's Fotography channel! I've got spoons and bowls and measuring cups, so it's time for *Serena Says* DIY!

Since there's no big bottle of glue, I'm sure you can tell we're not making slime. Ha-ha—actually, if you want to see my mom lose it COMPLETELY, just mention the Slime Incident of 2019. It was NOT cool. Today's *Serena Says* Public Service Announcement reminds viewers to NEVER leave your slime out on the bed because if your mom takes your comforter and puts it in the washer . . . well, it's all bad, that's all I have to say.

Anyway—nope, we're not making cookies either. I've got coconut oil, and shea butter, which I use in my hair. These are charcoal tablets from the health food store. I've also got cocoa powder, without any sugar in it. This bottle is turmeric, and this little bag is spirulina powder Mom uses for her smoothies. This is arrowroot powder—you can get it from the grocery store. It's what people use for baking if they're gluten-free. We got it for my sister's friend Sharyn.

Are you stumped yet?

For today's DIY, we're making my friend El's natural

eyeliner and eye shadow! Here's an Egypt fact: Did you know that in ancient Egypt they made eye shadow out of copper—for green—and lead? Men and women wore it because it was supposed to have magic powers. Well, we're not using lead and copper, but El made this for our class project—and it works.

Before we start, Serena says safety first. Be careful with your eyes—and have some eye drops right next to you, just in case you get eye shadow in them. Nothing we use is dangerous, but anything you get in your eyes will irritate them and make them water.

Let's start! Into your bowl, put **one-fourth teaspoon of arrowroot powder**. It will make the eye shadow really smooth and pastel, and you can always add more to make a different shade.

Next add **one-fourth teaspoon of whatever spice powder for color.** You can mix up the spirulina and turmeric to make different shades. The cocoa powder and charcoal are brown and black, obviously. We haven't figured out how to get red or blue yet, but you can experiment.

Mix your dry powder so there's no clumps, then add **one-fourth teaspoon of shea butter** and **one-fourth teaspoon of coconut oil.** I stuck the coconut oil in the microwave for five seconds, so it mixed better. Put your eye shadow in a little jar with a lid or recycle an empty lip gloss pot.

Tie a ribbon around it, and boom! You're done!

The eye shadow still mostly looks kind of crumbly and powdery, but the oil helps it stay on. Dip a cotton swab into your eye shadow, and then tap off all the extra before you put it on your eyes, or you can also put it on with your finger, which is what I did.

So that's it! We're done.

People LOVE to get homemade gifts because it means you thought about them for more than five minutes. I love MAKING homemade gifts, because DIY is good for the brain—stirring stuff lets your hands work while your brain goes offline and cools down or figures things out.

Does crafting stress you out, or give you Zen vibes? What do you like to make? What do you want to see me make next? Serena says makers are AMAZING, and DIY is doable—so find a project and jump in!

That's my story, and I'm out.

27

All the Same and Totally Changed

"I'M GLAD WE'RE DOING this outside. This glue reeks," Lani muttered, leaning forward as she pulled the fabric cover of our Egypt book tight against the cardboard beneath.

"Well, it's better than breaking another needle," Eliana said, dragging her metal ruler down the flattened fabric, making the thick glue below smooth and bubble-free.

"We need to find out how much it costs to replace your mom's sewing stuff, El," I said, moving the glue gun away from Lani's arm. "I know she said she didn't need us to pay for it, but four needles is kind of a lot. Two pieces of canvas over this kind of foamboard is too thick to sew with a regular sewing machine."

"It's fine. It's going to look amazing," Eliana repeated. She'd been saying that ever since we'd had to change our cover plans, and Lani and I had kind of freaked out a little. Lani didn't want to change plans in the middle of the project, and I just wanted everything to be perfect. Eliana's mom saved the day when she found some thick foamboard and brought out her glue gun.

We glued the last bit of fabric on the back cover, and Lani stretched out the fabric again. I unplugged the glue gun and put it on the table to cool while Eliana centered her ruler again.

"How's your vlogging thing going?" Eliana asked. "You should take pictures of this so you can do a DIY on how to make a book cover."

"Aw, *man*!" I looked at the glue gun and groaned. "I should have filmed us. That would have been really good. I would have had to edit out how badly we screwed up the first one, but . . . yeah, this would've made a great DIY show."

"You have a vlog?" Lani raised her eyebrows. "What's your setup like?"

I shrugged, feeling shy. "Well, it's nothing high tech. Just my mom's old laptop."

"She makes really cute vlogs, though," Eliana

put in. "She showed how she made her WinterFest project."

"You know what, though . . ." Lani folded the sticky fabric under the edge of the cardboard and tightened the corner. "You could still film us for the project."

"Film us doing what?" I asked. "When we put everybody's pages in the book? That'll take, like, five minutes. We're not doing that much in class."

"No, I mean, you could film everyone—and have everybody talk about the project." Lani glanced at me, then looked down, picking off the glue that had stuck to the ruler's edge. "We could turn it in with our book."

"Oh, you mean like interview everyone? Huh." I chewed on my lip, thinking. "That might be *really* good. I could ask everyone a few questions and show Mr. Van my interview skills."

"And we could get even more extra credit," Eliana pointed out.

"Oh, let's do it. Let's definitely do it," Lani decided. "Serena, when can you get this organized?"

And that was that. Lani, Eliana, and I had put our heads together and made plans. And now the weekend was over.

The Monday after break usually felt like six years had passed since we'd been at school. We'd missed three days, plus the weekend, and most everyone was zonked—but I kept looking at the door, drumming my fingers in anticipation. Where was she?

My classmates yawned as the happy morning announcement music played on the TV. "Good *morning*, Brigid Ogan Middle School! Welcome to morning announcements!" Our vice-principal held up jazz hands on the screen.

Ugh. It was still too early for Mrs. Henry's hyper energy. After the usual boring announcements—the Running Club was meeting at lunch, Crochet Club was rescheduled to tomorrow, and all eighth graders needed to turn in their PATH forms by Thursday—I waited for Mrs. Henry to give us a special thought for the day, but instead, she said, "And now we'll welcome an old friend to our morning announcement studio to take us out. JC?"

"Wait, did she say JC?" Eliana asked.

A slow grin warmed me as I straightened. *This* was what I'd been waiting for.

My classmates sat forward and applauded as JC moved into camera range, wearing a black and gold Minnie ears hoodie—a gift from her aunt Gina—and a big, cheesy grin. At least, JC's eyes were scrunched up like she was grinning. We could only see her eyes, and the bridge of her nose behind the antiviral mask she was wearing.

JC sat down next to Mrs. Henry and waved. "Good morning, Brigid Ogan! I'm baaack!"

Our class was applauding and hooting so loudly, we missed part of what she was saying. Even Mr. Van was smiling, though like me, he'd already known what was coming.

"—for thinking of me while I got hooked up with my new kidney. I'm back at school for half days for now, but I'm super happy about it, and I get to go to WinterFest next week! So I'll be seeing you guys around. And remember"—her cheeks squinched her eyes even more—"be respectful, be responsible, and be kinder than necessary, because, Brigid Ogan, you're the bomb. I'm JC Gerardo—"

"And I'm Vice-Principal Henry. Hope you enjoyed the show. Stay classy, Brigid Ogan!"

Everyone cheered, finally settling when Mr. Van stood at the door, holding up his hand for quiet. Just as he started to speak, JC herself opened the door. 6A lost it all over again.

There were squeals and cheers as everyone rushed

up to her to say hello. The antiviral mask was a bright-blue reminder that JC's body wasn't perfect yet, so instead of hugging her, people patted her on the back or squeezed her shoulders from behind. JC just ate it up, grinning like she was in a parade, her eyes bright.

Across the aisle, Lani caught my eye and smiled. We hung back from the rest of the class, waiting our turn, since we'd seen JC only yesterday. Only Lani and I knew how hard JC had been working on her parents to get them to let her go back to school so soon. She'd had to pinky-swear promise to go for a whole week with no backtalk, and she'd had to catch up with all of her homework. When they still seemed reluctant, I'd suggested that she promise her mom and dad—in front of Julia, Lani, and me as witnesses—to take all her medications, and not even be late with one, ever, ever again. And though JC rolled her eyes and complained about how her parents trusted us more than they trusted her, we all knew that the Gerardos were relieved that things were finally getting back to normal. Or, as normal as JC could be, as she waved at her classmates like a guest celebrity.

"Hey, peeps!" JC's face was flushed as she dumped

her backpack at the desk in front of me. "Can you believe I'm so pathetic that I'm happy to be back at school?"

I'd forgotten how much JC seemed to move all the time—tossing her hair, bouncing her leg, and turning to roll her eyes when Mr. Van said something weird. She kept passing Lani notes, and Lani, who was very serious about her math, just flapped her hand at JC to leave her alone. I was impressed when JC turned around and paid attention. Lani sometimes seemed like she was prickly, but I had learned this weekend at Eli's house that she was just honest and straightforward—and when she said no, she meant it. I needed to be more like that. People like JC took Lani seriously.

Social studies was . . . kind of surprising. Mr. Baumgartner had started JC on her own project, since the plan had been for her to come back to school in January, so she was curious about what we were working on in groups. She sat at our table as Cameron took out his trifold poster and started going over the pencil lines on his cartouches with a fat black marker. He'd chosen to do his poster on the names of the Egyptian gods, with drawings of the gods, and a winding blue line across all three panels of the poster to represent the Nile.

"*You're* doing extra credit, Cameron?" JC asked him. "*You?*"

"It's not extra credit." I jumped in before Cam could get defensive—or worse, distracted. "It's group credit. Cameron's just making sure we get our A."

JC turned to me, a funny expression on her face. "I still kind of can't believe you're the group leader," she said. "You!"

I opened my mouth to say something like, "No one else wanted to," but Mateo spoke first.

"Why would you say that? Serena has good ideas," he said, looking up from the thick, hard-back thesaurus on the table in front of him. He'd been working on his Nile Facts Rap for the past two weeks. "She got Mr. Van on our side too."

JC's eyes widened, and she wiggled her eyebrows at me.

"What?" I asked, but JC only winked and bent to work on her social studies.

When the bell rang, JC stood up and raised her hands. "And that's a wrap, people. I'm out!" Everyone laughed. As we left the library and headed toward the cafeteria, a few teachers gave JC non-hugs again, and Lani, who was hurrying to grab food before going to band, waved her clarinet music and said she'd be over at JC's later. I waited with JC while she collected her project, and more assignments from teachers whose classes she'd miss. Then I got a pass from Mr. Van to walk JC out to the front parking lot while she waited for her mother.

"So, Mateo Rodríguez, huh?" JC said, hiking her book bag on her shoulder as we went down the front steps and into the drizzly, overcast day.

"Huh? What about Mateo?" I asked, peering across the parking lot. Just ahead of us, Harrison was walking across the slanted white parking lines to a four-door gray car. He'd missed school before Thanksgiving, too, and I wondered again if something new was happening with his brother, Lance. The trunk popped open as Harrison approached the car, and he put his briefcase inside and slammed it before hurrying around to the passenger side.

"I think he likes you, that's what," JC said, sounding smug.

I blinked, tuning back in. "What? *WHAT*? Mateo? No, he doesn't."

Tightening her scarf, JC widened her eyes. "Didn't you hear what he said?"

"That I'm a good group leader?" Harrison was

dragging his seat belt across his body now.

JC shook her head. "Those were the words he said, but that's not what he *meant*," she told me. "Boys don't say it like that."

I rolled my eyes. Like JC would know what every boy in the world did. "He doesn't like me like that," I told her. "He just knows I'm not going to get him a bad social studies grade."

JC's brows wriggled like a pair of hooked fish. She was getting *really* good at making faces with only the top half of her face. "That's what *you* think, but you'll see," she sang mysteriously, then added, "You coming over after school? I think Lani and I are finally going to finish our magnets today."

The gray car had made a U-turn and drove out of the parking lot. "Um . . . I don't think so," I said slowly. "I think I might have something to do."

"With Mateo, huh? Text me deets!"

I put one hand over JC's face mask where her mouth would be, and with the other, gently smacked her forehead. "Wait, she's babbling again, must be a fever. Good thing you're going home, JC. Your brain is *definitely* sick."

And right on time, Mrs. Gerardo drove up, rescuing her daughter from laughing herself to death at my expense. JC rolled down the window and screamed something about Mateo that got swept away on the wind. I stuck out my tongue, then waved with both arms as the car pulled away.

JC was completely ridiculous—annoying and hilarious too. Even if we weren't *best* friends, I was glad we could still *be* friends.

❧ 28 ❧

Asked and Answered

I HITCHED UP MY backpack and got off the bus at the corner of Grant Street. Fallon had stayed after school for Running Club, so I was alone cutting through the rows of cars nosed into parking slots, watching my breath make clouds around my head.

I'd asked Mom if I could visit her at work. Instead of the questions I'd expected, she'd just said, "Text me when you get here," so I sent a quick message, shivering as I hustled through the warm foyer of the Behavioral Health Center's administration building and headed for the lobby.

My footsteps slowed. Harrison wasn't by himself this time, but sitting hunched over next to a burly man, who was hunched over in just the same way.

They both had their elbows on their knees, their chins resting on their fists, and were talking quietly. At least, the man was talking, the dangling cord to his earbuds making me wonder if he was on a phone call. Harrison was just sitting there, staring out into space.

I hesitated. This might have been a bad idea; just because Harrison was kind of my friend again didn't mean I really *knew* him. What if he was embarrassed to talk to me in front of his family? What if he was mad that I'd just showed up? Maybe I should go visit Mom's office for real. Harrison probably already had all the company he needed.

Just as my feet untangled themselves for the first step backward, Harrison's eyes met mine. His expression was surprised, then something else that made the muscles holding his mouth tight loosen and curl up at the corners.

"Hobbit," Harrison said, as if he wasn't quite talking to me.

"Mutant—um . . ." I flicked a quick glance at the man—his father? "Harrison."

"You again," Harrison said.

"Pretty much," I said, balancing my backpack on the table in front of me. I wavered. Should I tell him the truth, or—? "So. Mom's at work. Again."

Harrison's smile twisted. "My brother, Lance, is here. Still."

I cleared my throat and looked at Mr. Ballard again. He wasn't even watching us, just sitting forward and rubbing the back of his neck with his hand. I took a seat in one of the cushy waiting room chair clusters, this one in front of a small table. After a moment, Harrison came over and sat down across from me.

I unzipped my backpack. "Want to play Agricola?" I asked, holding out a wooden pig.

Harrison looked from the pig to my bag. "You carry toy pigs in your backpack?"

I rolled my eyes and pulled out the game board, and the barnyard boards. "I went home to get the game, Mutant. I don't just carry the pieces around."

Harrison looked mystified as I pulled out the rest of the animals, tiles, cards, and markers that we would need. "I've never even heard of this game."

"No problem," I said, tossing him the rule book. "It's easy."

"Easy?" Harrison shook his head at the pages of instructions. "I should have known Hobbits wouldn't play anything normal like chess."

"Chess? Bo*ring.*" I rolled my eyes. "That's such a Mutant game."

"Son?" Mr. Ballard approached the edge of our table, carrying Harrison's briefcase. He set the case down next to Harrison, giving me a nod. "I'm going back upstairs. You can change your mind and join us at any time, but you look like you're getting comfortable here—?"

"Yeah, thanks. I'm good," Harrison said, keeping his eyes on the fine print in the rule book.

Mr. Ballard paused a moment, as if giving Harrison a chance to say something—maybe introduce me?—and then smiled down at his son, who was completely wrapped up in reading and ignoring him. "Well, if you change your mind, you know where we are." He rubbed his knuckles on Harrison's head—ducked back as Harrison swatted at him, then winked at me, before crossing the lobby toward the bank of elevators.

I watched Mr. Ballard walk away, a little weirded out at how he even moved like a much bigger version of the mutant Ballard across from me. I wondered if something had happened today or recently that had made things worse for Harrison's brother, and if that was the reason they were all here again today.

I wished it wasn't totally nosy to ask, but I could just imagine Mom glaring at me. Some things, like diagnoses and other people's troubles, were absolutely off-limits, and I decided to keep my nosiness to myself.

I glanced back at Harrison to find him watching me, his expression very carefully no expression at all.

"You should just ask," he said, balancing a little cattle token on top of another cow's back. "You know you want to know, so just get it over with."

"Harrison—" I bit my tongue, hard, to stop the automatic denial. I wasn't going to make the same mistake two times. I *did* want to know—a lot—but was asking the right thing to do? I looked at Harrison hard, frowning over the puzzle of his face. Was there a question that really needed asking?

Just ask.

"Okay." I gave the answer to myself and said it again to Harrison. "Okay. I'm asking."

Harrison blinked, like he wasn't expecting this. He put down the cow he was fiddling with and crossed his arms. "So?"

"Um." Nerves tiptoed my skin, and I rubbed my arms uncomfortably. It was one thing to want to know details about Harrison's brother and his family, but asking them straight out? "Um, so I want to know . . . wait. First, are you okay, Harrison? I mean, in a way you're not okay, because Lance is here, and I know that's kind of a lot, and I know you sometimes miss school, and I know you missed senate last week, which probably bugged you, since your friend Mrs. Henry didn't get to tell you how awesome you are, but I know your parents spend a lot of time here, and you stay with your grandparents sometimes, which is probably fine, too, but not normal . . . so," I took a big breath, wincing at Harrison's stunned expression. "Sorry—I mean, I know you're not *okay*-okay, but I'm just checking: Are you mostly okay? Is there something I can do? To help?"

"Uh . . ." Harrison avoided my eyes, fiddling with the game pieces. He balanced another stack of cows, then cleared his throat. "Yeah, I'm okay," he said, then looked at me and shrugged. "I mean, I'll feel much better when I completely own you at whatever this game is, but I'm good."

"Yeah, right," I said, suddenly embarrassed, and a little disappointed. After working hard to make sure I was ready to listen, Harrison wasn't . . . saying anything. Maybe I hadn't asked right. "Whatever,

Mutant. You can forget about owning anything. You don't even know how to play."

"I'll figure it out," Harrison said, and bent back over the rules.

It's hard to teach a game and play it at the same time. It mostly went okay, but Harrison eventually got irritated with the rule book—and probably tired of me reminding him of things—and dug into his briefcase for one of the same legal pads he'd used for the Red Ribbon stuff.

"What? I need to take notes," he said, at my disbelieving glance.

"Why do you carry a briefcase, anyway?" I asked, leaning to the side so I could see the contents. I remembered JC's claim that he had nothing but little pieces of paper inside with my name on them. "What do you have in there?"

"Just all the stuff I need," Harrison said. He paused.

Before I could ask what kind of stuff a giant Boy Mutant might need, Harrison slid out a gray rectangle from an inner pocket. "Want to see something?" He turned the rectangle around, and I saw a framed picture of a shorter, thicker Harrison standing by a waterfall with another big boy. Lance was even taller than Mr. Ballard, and his curly hair was even bigger than Harrison's. His grin was just the same.

"You guys climbed a mountain?"

"Well, part of one," Harrison said, turning the frame back toward himself. "We went camping at Big Basin by Santa Cruz for Lance's graduation. Dad took us hiking up to Berry Creek Falls."

"Cool."

"It was a good trip." Harrison buffed the glass with his sleeve. "Lance is a really good climber. He climbs Half Dome at Yosemite every summer." Harrison paused, then corrected himself. "I mean, he *climbed* it. Before. Last summer he was at college, so he didn't, but he told me his medication messed up his balance anyway." Harrison shrugged. "That's why he stopped taking it, I guess. He has," Harrison said the name like he was reading it from a medical book, "mixed-features bipolar disorder."

"Oh." I wasn't sure what that was, but I knew that when Mom's patients stopped taking their drugs, it usually meant they spent time back at New Vista until their bodies learned how to feel right taking them again. Sometimes they felt worse than they had before they'd taken medication to begin with. "I hope they find Lance a different drug."

Harrison shrugged. "That's what they're supposed

to be doing. It isn't working, though. Lance was supposed to climb Vernal Falls with Dad and me this year, but I don't think we're going."

I tucked my fingers in a fist to keep from chewing on my nails. Harrison sounded sad. "That sucks. Maybe you can plan to hike something else. Something flat?"

Harrison put the picture back into his briefcase and sighed. "Maybe."

"What else do you do? With your brother, I mean? It's kind of cool you hang out."

Harrison shrugged. "We play games that don't have sheep in them."

I shook my head, sighing. "Dude, you do not know what you're missing, then."

Harrison returned to his pad of paper. "Okay. Let me get this straight. I can *only* make two moves on each turn . . . ?"

"Rena-Bean? I'm ready to go." Mom had her bag over her shoulder and was shrugging into her coat. She smiled at Harrison. "Harrison, you're welcome to come home with us and have something to eat. Your mom and dad said they could pick you up from our house."

"Come over, Harrison," I whispered loudly. "Mom will get us pizza."

Mom rolled her eyes and whispered back, "We are having sourdough toast and minestrone." In a normal voice she added, "You can make mini pizzas from the sourdough if you want, but you're on your own. Soup's already made, and we're not ordering out."

Harrison gnawed his lower lip. "Is Lance up?"

Mom nodded. "Last I saw, he was sitting in the activity room with your dad."

Harrison picked up his briefcase and looked at me. "Thanks for the game, but I think I'm going to ask Lance if he knows a hike we can take that's not as steep."

A little disappointed, but also a little bit relieved, I looked carefully at Harrison's expression again. For once, he didn't look like he was making fun of me. "Maybe your dad knows a place," I said as I tucked the last pig away.

Harrison nodded, looking determined now. "See you tomorrow."

On the way out, Mom put her arm around me and squeezed. "I feel like I should get a briefcase," she said. "Harrison looks more like an adult than I do."

"You don't need a briefcase," I told her, hugging her back. Mom didn't have to carry reminders of the people she needed. "You've got me."

Mom laid her cheek on top of my head. "That's all right, then," she said.

And it was.

SERENA|SAYS

What's up, World? It's your girl Serena! Welcome back to my vlog, and welcome to those of you who just heard I have one. Today *Serena Says* is reporting LIVE from the Brigid Ogan WinterFest!

[applause]

We have a little time before the basket raffle, so I'm here with Brigid Ogan community members Cameron, Ally, Mateo, Eliana, and Lani in front of this amazing Nile project book on display here in the library. Cameron, say hello to our viewers, and tell us the story of how you ended up doing this amazing poster.

"Uh . . . hi! Yeah, um, so, I did this poster for, um, extra credit for our group."

It's really good. Tell us a little more. What made you put that little cat on the bottom?

"I made a mummy first. It was papier-mâché, and I rubbed dirt into it so it looked really old and gross . . . but then I thought it would look better as a page in the book, so I drew a cat for the poster because people in Egypt liked cats."

Thanks, Cameron. Hi, Mateo, will you share with us one of the rhymes from the book?

"Yeah, so one of my facts was about pyramids, right?

So, okay, let me get a beat—

'My rhyme drops deep, as deep as a tomb—

(That's a box made outta rocks deep in the Earth, a room.)

In Egypt where I'm rappin', in a pyramid state of mind

The treasures that you're trackin' will drop a curse on your behind.

Imhotep, you'd better step back and check it—

130 is the count, though a king still tried to wreck it.

Al-Aziz gave it up, and you'd better give up too.

Five tons of limestone brick—the pyramids will flatten you.'"

Nice. I think that's my favorite one, Mateo. Hi, Ally! Will you tell our viewers about your part of the project?

"Yeah! Um, hi, one of my facts is about ancient Egyptian inventions. So I made a page about toothpaste, because the Egyptians invented it."

Cool! Did you try to brush your teeth with it?

"Well, I only mostly made the recipe. My mom wouldn't let me buy iris root, because it was kind of expensive, so I used rock salt and crushed mint and crushed peppercorns, and left out the iris. And it was SO gross—it was all salty and gritty and the pepper burned my mouth . . . but it also made my teeth feel really slick. So I guess it worked?"

Um, I guess? Eew, though, right? Ally, thanks for trying it out for us. Eliana, welcome to *Serena Says*. Viewers, Eli made the amazing eye shadow she's wearing—and you can check out my DIY vlog from two weeks ago to learn how! So, Eli, tell us about putting the book together.

"Okay, so, we were going to use my dad's laminating machine to do the pages, but then Cameron's pages were, like, 3D, right? And you can't really laminate papier-mâché. SO, Lani said we should just, like, make a real book, like they do at publishing companies, with a sewing machine. We watched a video about how to make a cover out of cloth, but then we broke a bunch of Mom's needles sewing it on her sewing machine, so we used a ton of glue. We punched in holes to lace the pages together, and we used three of my dad's C-clamps and a brick to weigh it down because it's so big, the book wouldn't lay down flat at first. But then, finally, it did!"

It looks great, like a real book.

"We are SO going to get an A!"

So, Lani . . . last but definitely not least! Tell the viewers what you loved about this project.

"Hi, everybody. This was really fun. One of my facts was about hieroglyphs, and my favorite page was making a sentence using all these little drawings. They're actually kind of pretty. I'm not very good at drawing, but I could make all the little symbols."

That's cool. The symbols were really neat, and I think they look great on the cover.

"You know the best thing about this project, though? Everybody did some, right? I mean, even though SOME PEOPLE fooled around a lot, everybody worked, too, and we are for sure getting an A. You're a good project manager, Serena. Not to be mean or anything, but sometimes people don't know other people are nice or whatever because they don't get to talk to them. It's been nice to talk to you more."

Oh, wow, Lani. Yeah, same. It's been nice to talk to you more too.

[pause]

Well, viewers, it's time for the raffle, so I'm going to bounce, but first, tell me what you think. Hit me with your comments in the Community tab and let me know—do you think we're going to get an A for this project or what? Have you ever done a project you thought you'd hate, but then found out you loved? Do you have a classmate who is kind of unexpectedly awesome? Or—hi, Harrison!—a Mutant classmate who is growing on you—kind of like mold? Serena says there are amazing people around—all you have to do is be yourself and you'll find them. Remember, stand up and speak out, be kinder than necessary, and let the world see your awesomeness.

This is Serena St. John. That's my story, and I'm out.

ACKNOWLEDGMENTS

With gratitude to JC, who let me pick her brain for all the details of her kidney transplant, and to my writing group—David Elzey, Suzi Guina, Sara Lewis Holmes, Jennifer Richter, and Sarah J. Stevenson—who so often let me borrow their voices. Finally, thanks to everyone in the transplant community—hospital support staff, nurses, doctors, donors, and recipients—who make sure people like me get to keep their little sisters, and who make extraordinary miracles appear ordinary every single day. Thank you, thank you, thank you.